Teach Me

sloan johnson

Teach Me
Copyright © 2014 by Sloan Johnson
Editing by Anna Coy
Cover Design by Sloan Johnson
Formatting by Pink Ink Designs https://www.facebook.com/PinkInkDesignsbyCassy

Dedication

This book is dedicated to everyone who has been cast aside simply because of who they are. Please know that you are loved and life can get better.

Chapter One

Somehow, I knew it would come to this. As the hands on the clock creep closer to eight, I resign myself to the fact that I am alone. All day, I've been forced to listen to families reuniting at the end of the school year while trying to hold onto a shred of hope that my father hasn't managed to turn everyone in my family against his disappointment of a son. Apparently, he has.

I start rifling through the totes I've spent the past week packing to determine what is and isn't essential. Had I been honest with myself sooner, I would have done this as I packed so I could make a hasty escape when reality slapped me in the face.

I take my time rolling and stuffing as many clothes as possible into my backpack and the duffel bag typically used for weekend trips. There's easily a thousand dollars' worth of clothes left in the clear plastic containers that I could have taken to one of the consignment shops if I had thought of it sooner. In hindsight, putting all of this crap on Craigslist would have been smart; at least then I would have had a bit of a nest egg going into the summer.

With my two bags, a laptop and my cell phone, which hasn't worked in over two months in hand, I turn back at the door, taking one last look at the life I'm probably leaving behind for good. It's the end of an eye-opening year; some of it good, some of it bad, and a little bit downright ugly. I'd like to think I'll come out of this a stronger man than I am today, but it's hard to stay optimistic when you come to the realization that everything you've been told your entire life is a fucking lie.

"Austin, you have to have *everything* out by eight," the uptight resident assistant reminds me as he passes my open door. Right now, I hate him. His parents carried all of his crap down to their rolling status symbol of an SUV while he spent the day reminding everyone of the policies that have been tacked on every bulletin board and sent in numerous emails over the past month. His family will be waiting for him at five after eight, probably so they can take him out to dinner to celebrate the end of another wonderful school year.

"Yep, got everything right here," I tell him as I pull the door shut to keep him from looking past me. Knowing my luck, he'll start asking questions I don't have answers to and that's the last thing I need. "As soon as I check out, I'll be out of your hair. Have a good summer."

"You too, Austin," he responds without the same prickly tone from a few moments ago.

Fat chance, but thanks. I don't say this out loud, of course, since that would lead to questions or yet another person telling me that it might not be as bad as I'm anticipating. Although I already miss Eric, my roommate from this year, I'm glad he left as soon as his last final of the semester was turned in. I'm not sure I could have handled the pity in his eyes if he saw me today. Plus, he is one of those people who is perpetually optimistic and I'm sick of hearing his pep talks on a daily basis.

Given the mood I'm in right now, I would likely take out my frustration on him because he's the one who somehow made me keep hoping that my parents would come around. And even if that were to happen, he would somehow wear down my defenses and offer for me to come home with his family for the summer. They're nice enough people, but they're all like him; they feel it's their civic duty to fix other people's problems and they'd refuse to see that there's no fixing this. If I think of it, I'll call him after shit settles down a bit and let him know I'm still alive.

Rather than turning right to the bank of elevators, I turn left toward the fire exit. Taking the stairs is going to suck with this much weight on my back, but the alternative is waiting who knows how long for the elevator with my classmates and their families. I'm really not in the mood to listen to them recap the school year and talk about what amazing trips they have planned for the summer.

Outside is more of the same chaos; families trying to cram everything into their vehicles, friends saying goodbye to one another, basically the world's way of dishing up one big middle finger to me. No one even notices the kid walking toward the lake with nothing but a bag on his back and one in his hands.

When I first moved to town, I loved the fact that my dorm was only a block from Lake Mendota. Late at night, I would follow the bike trail away from the crowds gathered on the terrace and sit in the darkness listening to the waves caress the shore. I won't go to my special spot tonight though, because I won't allow my sanctuary to be tainted by what I'm feeling right now. The lake, as it turns out, is about the worst place for someone trying to avoid people. The terrace is filled with families having drinks by the shore as they wait for tonight's entertainment to finish setting up on the stage.

I make it about ninety minutes before my arm feels like it'll fall off at any given moment. Grabbing as many of my possessions as possible seemed like a good idea. Turns out, I wouldn't know a good idea if it bit me in the ass.

Thunder rumbles in the distance, warning me that it's time to stop wishing and start planning. The alternative is even more weight when my bags become waterlogged. I manage to make it two blocks before the first drops slap me in the face. I sprint toward a wooden pedestrian tunnel two blocks up as the rain starts falling in sheets around me. Sore and out of breath, I drop my duffel to the ground before easing myself onto the broken concrete.

"You waiting on the bus?" I look up and see a man, probably not much older than myself, glaring down at me. His long hair is twisted into dreadlocks and the thin cotton covering his body can barely be called clothing. "If so, you'd be better off waiting in the shelter. They won't wait around on a night like tonight."

A lump forms in my throat as I search for the truth. Even as I walked around aimlessly, I somehow managed to avoid putting a voice to my problems. In the end, I can't do it. There's no way I'm going to let the dozen or so transients taking cover know that I'm the new kid on the block while I'm carrying around a laptop and cell phone that could easily be pawned. That's exactly what will happen with the phone, but I need to keep my computer safe. "No, not waiting on anything but the rain to stop."

I tuck the duffel beneath my knees and slide the backpack off my shoulders. The guy with the dreads whispers something into his girlfriend's ear before easing himself onto the ground beside me. My body stiffens as I watch him tap a cigarette out of the crinkled pack before he offers me one. I consider accepting even though I've never smoked a day in my life because I don't want to upset him by rejecting his generosity.

The young couple sits next to me, talking in hushed tones as the wind howls through the tunnel. None of us are staying dry, but it's better than nothing and we're only wet instead of soaked to the bone. With the way my year has gone so far, that'd lead to starting my summer with a bout of pneumonia and a stack of medical bills I have no hope of paying.

I pull the nearly-worthless phone and a set of cheap earbuds out of the front pocket of my bag and stuff them into my ears so I'm not tempted to eavesdrop on their conversation. I quickly realize my mistake when I see them gaping at me even more now.

"What's your deal?" the girl asks. Her clothes are almost as tattered as her boyfriend's, but her chocolate brown dress has an artsy, vintage feel to it. In fact, the closer I look at her outfit, I don't think they're tattered by repeated wear so much as purposely distressed to look older than they are. The differences in the two of them are subtle, but there nonetheless. It fascinates me, and then annoys me a bit because I'm doing exactly what I don't want them doing to me: judging them based on how they look.

She pulls a sketchpad out of her messenger back and begins studying my face as she puts the pencil to paper. As the lead scratches each line, I wonder how she sees me. Will the resulting sketch show my naïveté and innocence? The pain I try to hide from the world? Or the little rich boy I look like with my L.L. Bean backpack and duffel bag? When I try glancing at her work in progress, she pulls the paper closer to her chest so I can't see. When I fidget, trying to get comfortable, she huffs in frustration, so I try to sit still. Why I give half a shit whether or not she's annoyed with me is a mystery.

"What do you mean?" I can't figure out if she's genuinely interested or trying to pry for information. Out here, I truly am on my own and I can't make the mistake of trusting anyone.

She continues sketching as the guy lights another cigarette, dividing his attention between the image on the page and my face. He mutters encouragement toward her before turning his attention to me. "Look, kid..." I bristle at the condescending tone in his voice. "You look lost and tonight's going to be a nasty one. Whatever you're trying to do, you should probably head back to your air-conditioned apartment and conduct your little social experiment when the weather clears."

"That'd be great, if I had an apartment, air conditioned or not." My eyes are cast toward the stained sidewalk. I try not to think about what causes the discoloration because it's most likely disgusting and most definitely unsanitary. "Contrary to what you might believe, not everyone who looks like me has parents who foot the bill for his every need."

I push myself off the ground, nearly clobbering the guy as I swing the backpack onto my shoulder. It seems I've reached a sort of purgatory where I don't fit into any of the worlds around me. I have no idea where I'll go, but anywhere is better than sitting here listening to him tell me all the ways I don't belong out here. I don't. I shouldn't be here. But the cold fucking truth is I don't exactly have much of a choice.

The other man kisses his girlfriend on the cheek before gracefully standing. I make it three steps into the rain before his fingers wrap around my arm. Not wanting to cause any more of a scene than I already have, I turn to face him. I don't punch him, as much as I want to because he has no fucking right to put his hands on me. Instead, I square my shoulders and hide the fear that has every hair on my body standing on end.

His blue eyes are framed with dark circles and premature age lines, but there's none of the critical judgment I expect to see. "Kid, if you're going to make it out here, you're going to have to toughen up. You're about as out of place sitting there as I would be walking into the Madison Club. That means people aren't going to trust you easily. Believe it or not, a lot of guys our age think it's fun and rebellious to stay out here. Basically, it's a way for them to say 'fuck you' to their pretentious parents. But I don't get that vibe from you. Come on and sit with us until the rain clears. Once it's not coming down quite so hard, I'll show you where you can stay as well as the spots you need to avoid at all costs."

"Why?" The desperate part of me wants to believe that he's doing this because he's a good man who knows how hard it is to take the first steps onto the street. The rest of me, the part that's been filled with misconceptions and stereotypes most of my life, figures he sees me as an easy mark; someone who will be easy to rob blind in the middle of the night. I know I should listen to my head, but it's filled with so much garbage right now that I do something I'll probably regret and allow him to lead me back into the makeshift tunnel.

"Because I've been where you are. I don't know *why* you're here when you should be there," he says, cocking his head toward campus. "Then again, I don't suppose it matters why or how, does it? The fact is, you're so far out of your comfort zone I'm not sure you would even know how to find it at this point. If you camp out at the wrong place, you're liable to get picked up or jumped and you seem like a decent kid other than the chip on your shoulder."

"I don't have a chip," I protest. Not once have I gone out of my way to be an asshole to him or his girl. I'm simply trying to protect myself in an unknown world.

"You do," he argues. "We all do and that's not entirely bad, either. Out here, we've all been screwed, either by our own choices or the shit hand life dealt us. What you need to figure out is how to keep the cause from pulling you under."

While my new life is one I never fathomed living, it's not all bad. Casey and Bree have officially taken me under their wings, almost like street parents. And yes, that's a real thing out here and age doesn't matter. When I had no clue where to go or what to do, they didn't ask questions before showing me how they survive from one day to the next. We walk around during the day talking about who's good and who to avoid out here, where to hang out and where to avoid like the plague. No matter what happens in my life, I'll never forget Casey for being the first person to accept me without knowing anything about me. To him, I'm just Austin. I'm not some rich kid with a silver spoon in my mouth, I'm not a disgrace to those around me, I'm just me. And dammit if that's not one of the best feelings in the world. The night I stepped out of the comfort of my dorm room, I thought my life was ending. In reality, I feel more alive than I have in years, all because I've stripped away the material bullshit that most of us use to assign value to our existence.

The past few nights have been spent sitting in dilapidated lawn chairs, listening to a Vietnam vet play classic rock tunes on his guitar while Casey and Bree draw inspiration from the world around them to create line sketches and paintings to sell to anyone willing to name a price. It seems everyone up here has some sort of skill that helps them make just enough money to eat and buy the necessities.

Tonight, we're dining on subs made from stale bread and produce that's reached its expiration date. It's the most I've had to eat at any one time since leaving the dorms. I'd give anything to have a few slices of lunch meat, but Casey made a good point when he said we're better off sticking to the food that won't kill us if it's starting to go bad.

Every morning, I leave my bags with Bree so I can fill out job applications. I have no work experience, no address and no contact phone number, so it doesn't come as a surprise that most managers don't want to take the chance on someone like me. That's why I've decided to see if I can borrow five dollars from Casey tomorrow morning. My plan is to take the bus to the mall, sell my useless phone and pick up a pre-paid one. Right now, having a way for potential employers to contact me is the only circumstance I have the power to change.

"Hey, Austin," Casey mumbles around a bite of his sandwich. "I got a line on some work for the weekend. It's going to be hot and miserable, but my buddy says the pay will be decent and in cash. You want in?"

"Hell yeah," I respond. It makes me feel better, knowing that he's making this offer to me instead of the other guys. He's known them longer, but I'm the one he's taking this chance on. "Any possibility it'll go longer than the weekend?"

"Probably not. His boss is a bit behind schedule and wants some extra hands to get back on track. He won't keep us around any longer than he has to. Besides, the guy he works for is way tough. Supposedly, if you don't have years of experience, he won't waste his time on you."

Bree gathers her stuff and makes her way from the concrete stairs we all call home to the sidewalk in front of one of the bars. It's her favorite spot because she can talk to passersby and there's a never-ending stream of inspiration for her drawings. Casey and I finish talking about the job, which turns out to be on a construction site, and join Bree after cleaning up.

Casey's told me time and again that being homeless isn't the same as being a pig. Part of the reason the cops don't give our little circle a hard time is because everyone respects one another as well as those more fortunate than we are. Even the belongings we don't take with us everywhere we go are neatly organized and stashed behind one of the decorative planters so there aren't piles of crap creating a blight in the area.

Chapter Two

David

I have been assured repeatedly that the house will be move-in ready by the end of August. That is still later than I would like since it will mean unpacking and organizing my home at the same time I am trying to make sure everything is in order for the first semester at a new school. I have been trying to stay positive, but that is nearly impossible when I pull into the driveway only to find a disorganized crew sitting around drinking coffee in what will eventually be the kitchen. And I can see this because they haven't gotten any further than rough framing. Not having doors and windows in place is one thing, but the fact that the house has no roof or OSB covering the studs raises my blood pressure to dangerous levels.

"Bill," I yell as I trudge through the muddy yard. The portly foreman freezes in place when he hears my voice, not because I intimidate him but because he knows he has been caught wasting time. Again. "Can I talk to you for a minute?"

Bill turns to his crew, barking out orders before joining me on the slab that will eventually be the garage. Like the house, it is framed when it should be close to finished. "Hey, David. I know what you're going to say, but before you do, I'm happy to say that we should be back on schedule by the end of the weekend. I authorized a couple of my guys to bring extra hands in so we can catch up. It's been a bitch this spring with all the rain."

He is making feeble excuses and we both know it. Yes, it has been a wetter than normal spring, but I signed the paperwork back in March, the same day I signed my contract with the university. This has always been my dream job and I have had money set aside to make a healthy down payment on the first place that will be completely mine. The day I took my first teaching job, I started saving back every dollar I could because I had never had anything new in my life. But it didn't make much sense to build a house in Mississippi when I couldn't wait to get out of there.

I pause when a young man who looks more ready for a day at the mall than on the worksite steps into the garage. He reminds me of every snotty kid who's walked through the doors of my classroom over the years, thinking he is something special because of the name sewn into the label of his designer clothes. Even from a distance, his hands look soft, as if they haven't seen a single day of hard work.

"Bill, I've heard it all before," I retort. The kid's doing his best to not make his eavesdropping obvious, but his efforts only draw attention to him. I would lay odds that he won't last the day. "And if that's the type of help you called in, I'm not so sure you are going to get anywhere. That one looks like he will spend more time on his cell phone than doing actual work."

The kid's shoulders slump and I feel like a jack-ass. I know as well as anyone that you can't make a fair assessment of people based on their outward appearances. However, knowing and doing are two completely different things, particularly when I have been proven right so many times in my career. The problem is, this kid didn't react the way most boys his age would. He didn't get defensive and tell me where I could put my holier-than-thou attitude. No, he looked like he had been punched in the stomach. Now, I have to swallow my pride and apologize to the kid.

"I'll tell you what; I don't have anywhere to be to-day, so I'm going to hang around to make sure work is getting done," I offer. Bill assesses me, practically snorting in disbelief. His eyes take in my appearance, from my gleaming white t-shirt to my new Columbia hiking boots. The boots will be wrecked after today, but it will be worth it to see some progress.

"You really think you're gonna be any more use to me than the kid over there?" Bill questions. "I don't know that one well, but if he works as hard as I think he will, he'll run circles around you. He's proba-bly more driven than half the crew. I ain't proud of that fact, but it's the truth. He and his buddy, both short-timers were the first ones here this morning and they've been antsy for somethin' to do since I pulled up."

"Point taken." I hold up my hands in surrender. "And if you're wrong about him that means you will have at least two work horses for the day."

The kid glances over his shoulder, seemingly pleased with my change in attitude. I'm not really a judgmen-tal dolt, it's just that I let my obsession with seeing this house completed get the best of me at times.

"You're seriously gonna hang around here and help out today?" Bill still doesn't understand that I will gladly spend the entire summer out here if it means moving in sooner. Actually, I might have to talk to Chad, the general contractor, about doing just that. It would take the whole 'having something all my own' to a whole new level, being able to look around knowing that I had a hand in the creation.

"Sure, why not? After all, I am the prick who's over her pissing and moaning about how behind things are." The kid gives me a crooked smile as he walks back toward the rest of the crew. I am tempted to run over to help him because his arms are seriously over-loaded with supplies. It appears the steady employees have designated him as the gofer, a job that will grow old quickly. "And just in case I am right about the kid and you are right about me, tell him to come over here and you can assign us whatever job you want. But don't think you need to go easy on either one of us."

Bill cocks an eyebrow, trying to figure out what I'm doing. *Good luck with that, I have no clue myself.* "So I'm s'posed to put two guys I know nothing about, both looking like they're closer to ready for a magazine photo shoot than a jobsite, together as a team? This is going to be a good thing how, exactly?"

"It'll be good because he and I both have something to prove, and there is no greater motivating force than someone telling you the you can't do something." I throw an arm over Bill's shoulders as we walk back to see what's going on with the different groups of men. I quickly pull back when the foreman's discomfort becomes apparent. Now that he realizes I'm not going anywhere, Bill barks out orders to each team, warning them that they won't be leaving tonight until everything is completed. If not for the apparent divide and conquer approach Bill has set up, I would have taken over the reins. For now, I will wait and see how things go.

The kid with the unruly brown hair doesn't seem thrilled that we will be working together and I can't say I blame him. What I felt when I realized I was unfairly judging him was nothing compared to the taste of my own medicine dished out by Bill. I motion for the kid to follow me so we can get to work. The first order of the day for most of us is working on putting the OSB on the walls. My hope is we'll be able to make some real progress by the end of today, but it is going to take a lot of work by everyone.

"What's your name?" I ask as we get to work on the back wall. The good news is that all of the lumber has been cut and numbered, so it should go up relatively quickly. The bad news is the day is already getting warm and the sun is still low in the sky. By the time we break for lunch, I have a feeling it will be miserably hot and sticky.

"Austin," he responds, not bothering to make eye contact with me. When he does look my way, I see a quiet determination in his eyes. He calls out to the guys who will be helping us, effectively dismissing me. I roll my shoulders and follow him. I pause for a moment to take in what will eventually be my backyard. Chad convinced me to take this lot because it's the largest in the subdivision and it butts up to a nature preserve, so I won't have to worry about anyone building directly behind me. If I close my eyes, I can almost hear the sounds of birds singing in the trees over the racket of saws, nail guns and bad pop music blaring from the work radios.

For three hours, four of us work on lining up each

sheet and securing it to the frame before moving on. My entire body already hurts, but I don't allow myself to slow down. Austin and I seem to be in a pissing contest of sorts, each trying to prove that we aren't the weak link on our crew. The result is nothing short of amazing, but I don't think Bill's fulltime employees appreciate the pace we are setting. They want to work at the rate they are used to, which isn't good enough anymore.

I want my house done and I am going to give up my summer to make sure it is. I will just have to get Chad on board with that idea, but that shouldn't be a problem. The two of us have been friends since the day we were assigned to the same team with AmeriCorps. That year taught us more about the value of hard work than any of these kids will ever understand, and it's time to put those lessons from long ago to good use. If he is half as smart as I remember him to be, he will realize that having one or two people on his crew pushing everyone else to work more efficiently will be a win-win for all parties.

Shortly after noon, everyone pulls up overturned buckets and toolboxes to break for lunch. Austin sits slightly off to the side, not making an effort to interact with the others. He also doesn't have a lunch with him, a fact that irritates me. Today is a long day filled with heavy labor and he's going to wind up going down if he doesn't get some food and water into his system.

For reasons I can't explain, I make my way over to him, quietly asking him to come with me. He hesitates when I tell him we're going to pick up something to eat and take a break from the humidity. "I didn't bring any money with me other than my bus fare," he says, obviously embarrassed by the admission.

"Good thing I'm not expecting you to treat then," I

respond. Rather than take part in a staring contest to see whose will will break first, I walk toward my car. There is no guarantee that he will follow me, but I recognized the moment of relief when I mentioned food right before he offered up his excuse. His pride may want to refuse my offer so no one considers him to be weak, but his need for nourishment will win. By the time I open the door to my car, Austin is jogging across the yard to catch up with me.

I do not know his story, but I don't need to. I can still remember the rumbling ache in my stomach that followed days without eating because it was right before payday. I took my first job the day I turned fourteen, and only waited that long because it was the law. My mother did the best she could to keep food on the table and a roof over our heads, but there were times it became impossible and I was limited to one meal a day and that only came because I qualified for free lunch. From the first paycheck until now, I have always made sure Mom has what she needs before worrying about myself. If I have anything to say about it, I will find a way to help Austin not have to live with those memories, at least for the time being.

Austin spends a long minute perusing the menu before trying to order nothing more than a small vegetarian sub; the cheapest item on the menu. After some prodding, I am able to convince him to get what he wants and he changes his order to a large club sandwich loaded with meat, cheese and every vegetable the deli offers. He keeps eyeing the shake machine and I urge him to get a milkshake as a reward for working at a nearly inhumane pace all morning in the heat.

It is apparent to me that Austin is uneasy with the silence while we eat, but he makes no move to strike a conversation, so I thank him for his help this morning and explain a bit about why I'm taking a much more hands-on approach. My theory is that if I share a bit of my own history, perhaps he will feel comfortable enough to tell me more about himself. If this was a hypothesis for a research study, I would be forced back to square one because he hasn't given me a single detail about his life, other than the fact that his friend got him this job. By the time we get into the car to get back to the house, I have more questions than answers but I vow to be patient and let him open up to me when he feels he can trust me.

The rest of the crew is already hard at work by the time we return from eating lunch and picking up three more cases of water. I am more relaxed than I have been in weeks and it is only partly because I'm starting to see the progress on the house that I have been waiting for.

Austin and I work side by side for the next few hours, developing the rhythm of a well-matched team. He's more relaxed, and every once in a while, I look over and see him stealing glances as well. When Bill comes around telling everyone it is time to clean up for the day, I am both relieved and disturbed. Every hour that has passed has helped to pull Austin out of his shell a bit more and I'm not ready for us to go our separate ways.

The kid makes me want to know everything about the pain I see in his eyes, the subtle tics when someone gets too close to him. My years of both learning and teaching have shown me that life is not always as it appears, but Austin takes that theory to a whole new level. He's not two different sides of a coin, it's like his sides are two parallel lines that can never intersect.

"Hey, Bill," I call out, setting down the nail gun to

chase after the foreman. The entire way, I try talking myself out of what I am about to do because it feels like a Hail Mary pass at the end of a football game. "I wanted to say thanks to everyone for the hard work today. I know I was a bit insufferable this morning and I would like to take everyone out for pizza to apologize."

"You weren't really that bad." Bill laughs. I follow him around the property as he surveys the work we've accomplished in one short day. He seems as impressed as I am with how everyone worked together to close in the walls. All of the interior rooms are framed and ready for the electricians and plumbers to come in. Honestly, it looks as if tomorrow will be a short day. "I figured we'd be working late into the night both today and tomorrow, but with the way you and the kid worked, I could almost give the crew a day off tomorrow if not for a pushy homeowner who's not content to sit on the sidelines."

"Then let me do something for the guys. They really kicked it into high gear today and I believe hard work should be rewarded." And I *really* want to spend some more time getting to know the twenty-year-old paradox but there is no way he will accept a meal from me twice in one day.

"If you insist." Bill shrugs. He turns his attention to the crew, informing them that dinner is on me. The announcement is met mostly with cheers, but Austin and one other guy are off to the side talking amongst themselves and they don't look pleased about the prospect of free pizza and beer. I watch from a distance, and Austin's friend almost seems upset about something. His arms are flailing around and his posture is defensive. Before I can make my way to them to find out what is going on, some of the guys from the crew call me over to them, thanking me for helping out.

Five minutes later, I see Austin and his friend walking down the street. The whole reason I cancelled on dinner with Chad and his family is leaving without a word to anyone.

The intelligent thing to do would be to let him walk away so I don't come across as some creepy pervert. After all, what thirty-five year old man is inexplicably drawn to someone so much younger than himself? I have never given much credence to age as a factor in attraction, but society does and always will. For that reason alone, I should let him walk away and forget about him. But I can't.

"Austin, where are you going?" I ask, running after him. Both men keep walking as if they didn't hear me, but I don't miss the way Austin's shoulders tense when I call after him. He knows what he is doing and he knows I know. If I have anything to say about it, he will not keep running for long. "Austin!"

This time, his steps falter. His buddy with the dreadlocks piled on top of his head says something to Austin before continuing to walk toward the bus stop. As I approach him, Austin steps onto the curb to avoid being hit by an oncoming car. My attention is diverted to the vehicle, wondering where they are going since there are no finished homes on this street.

"Hey, aren't you going to join us for pizza and beer?" I ask, more breathlessly than I care to admit. My exercise routine has become a thing of the past in recent months. Between getting ready to move and finishing out the school year down in Mississippi, I haven't had the time or energy for the gym. Yet another reason it will be beneficial for me to help out on the house this summer.

"Nah, I should probably get going," he sighs. "It takes a while to get back to where I'm staying by bus and I don't know the routes all that well."

"I can give you a ride," I offer. "Come on, you've earned a night out." Austin shirks away from me when I take a step closer. Whatever happened to this young man, it has left his soul with festering wounds and I want to be the one to help him heal. That notion makes no sense whatsoever because I am not the person anyone turns to when they are in need of nurturing.

"It's okay." Austin kicks the dirt beneath his feet. "It's been a long day and I'm beat."

Understandable but not acceptable. "You need to eat, Austin," I urge.

"You're not going to give up, are you?" The corner of Austin's mouth quirks slightly and I know I'm breaking through that protective exterior.

"No, I'm not," I confirm. "The sooner you realize that I do not give in easily, the better off we will both be. Now, are you joining us or not?"

Austin chews on the corner of his mouth nervously. "Depends on where you're going. Like I told you earlier, I'm only twenty, so a lot of places are out of the question."

The excuse is insubstantial and we both know it. If we were going to a bar for a night of wings and beer, he may not be able to join, but very few restaurants will deny anyone entrance based on their age. I cock my head to the side rather than dignify him with an answer. He will either follow or he won't, but either way I am ready to get off my feet and grab an ice-cold beer.

When Austin opens the passenger-side door as I turn the key in the ignition, I offer him a satisfied smile, but refuse to make a big deal over the fact that he changed his mind.

Chapter Three

Austin

I'm not at all surprised when David reaches for my arm as I pass him in the crowded restaurant. He pulls out the chair next to his own and I sit, telling myself that it's easier to go with the flow than draw unnecessary attention to myself. And that's a damned lie because David is a taste of reality in a theoretical world.

Every time he touches me, my nerves come to life and I know that my father was dead wrong when he said I only think I'm gay. Believe me, I highly doubt there are many straight boys out there having the type of thoughts that are running through my head. That doesn't mean I have cojones enough to do anything about it. Hell, there's a good chance I'm mistaking David's generosity for flirtation, in which case it'd truly suck to make a move and be shot down.

The rest of the crew fills in around the table and the

waitress brings three pitchers of beer. I flag her down and ask for a soda, more because I don't think it'd be wise to have my senses impaired when I get back to the park tonight than because of my age. I haven't had a night of real sleep since my last night spent in the dorms. Out on the streets, it's dangerous to fall into a deep, restorative sleep and the fatigue is already starting to set in. I have no clue how people like Bree and Casey do this week after week, month after month, and don't crumble. Maybe Casey was right the first night when his first assumption of me was that I don't have what it takes to survive in their world.

David relaxes into his seat, casually resting his arm on the back of my chair. I can feel the gentle pressure of his arm across my shoulder blades and I have to remind myself that we're in public. Even after a long day in the nasty heat, I can smell David's cologne mixed with his musk and I feel pressure building behind my jeans. The longer he stays in my personal space, the more comfortable I feel and that's dangerous because I can't think of too many things better than leaning into his side.

"Hey, Austin. Any chance you're lookin' for something to last the summer?" Bill asks as he shovels more pizza than should be humanly possible into his mouth. The man is a disgusting pig, but I bite back my reaction to him because he's just offered me the world. Okay, so that might be an exaggeration, but to a kid living on the streets, the idea of having a steady job to go to every day is amazing. And depending on the pay, there's a chance I might be able to bust my ass enough to pay this fall's tuition.

"Uh, yeah... I, uh..." *I've apparently lost the ability to speak.* I take a moment to gather my thoughts. "Yes, sir. I've been trying to find a job, but so far nothing's come up. Of course, it'll depend on the bus route because I don't have a car right now."

No one here needs to know that my father took the keys to my car before shoving my ass on a Greyhound at the end of spring break. Until that moment, I had been one of the lucky ones because a lot of freshmen have to rely on either public transportation, bicycles or mopeds to get around campus. Before the shit hit the fan, my father was more than willing to pay for my parking permits because he didn't want me to risk being late for anything. After, he couldn't have cared less because he wasn't about to continue supporting my sinful lifestyle. Seriously, that's what he said to me as I got out of the car at the bus stop. It could be worse, I suppose; he could have refused to get the bus ticket and then I would have had to leave everything behind and I'd have been living on the streets in small-town Minnesota.

"We'll help you figure that out," Bill promises me. "Good help's hard to find and I could use about a half-dozen more like you. Are you in school?"

My body stiffens, not wanting to answer that question. If I say yes, he might not want to bring me on board since it'd be temporary work, but if I say no, I'm either lying to him or subconsciously giving up on my dreams in life. Instead of choosing either option, I excuse myself from the table and hurry to the restroom. It's the cowardly thing to do, but there truly was a moment when I thought I might lose my dinner. I lean against the sink with my head bowed, wondering if this is really happening to me. Casey told me that his buddy told him there was no chance of this turning into anything more than a weekend of hard work for cash pay. That causes the guilt to fester in my gut because I'm the one being given a chance when Casey is the only reason I'm even here. I think about turning down the offer so there aren't any issues with my new friend, but quickly realize just how stupid that would be. And really, Casey can't be too upset since he's the one who told me that the first rule of making it on the streets is to look out for yourself. That's exactly what I'm doing. I splash some water on my face, spend a long minute staring into the mirror trying to figure out what in the hell happened to the life I had mapped out, and then walk back into the restaurant.

"Everything okay?" David asks when I return to the group. I nod, taking a long drink of my soda. Bill's off talking to one of the guys who's getting ready to take off for the night. "Look, I haven't talked to Bill about this yet, but I am going to be working on the house for the summer. I suppose you could say that I am a bit of a control freak when it comes to certain things and I need to know that I will have a roof over my head before winter. I could give you a ride, if you are interested. That way you don't have to worry about getting lost or missing a transfer on the bus."

I feel his arm settle at my back again, but this time, David allows his fingers to lightly graze my biceps. It would be so easy to give myself over to whatever it is that this man is offering me, but I can't allow that. I've already allowed Casey and Bree to start breaking down the walls keeping me safe, and they just want to be my friends. Nothing about the way David leans in toward me gives the indication that he's asking for friendship. What he wants is something my heart tells me I desperately need in my life, but this time, I have to listen to my head.

"That's very generous of you," I say. I lean forward to grab another slice, hoping he won't be sitting there so casual and sexy when I lean back. "But I can't put you out like that. I have to get used to taking the bus at some point. Might as well be now."

It seems David is incapable of taking the subtle hint and I feel the warmth of his palm on my shoulder blade. Unlike me, he's obviously confident enough with his sexuality to make blatant passes in the company of people we barely know while I'm digging my fingers into the seat of my chair to keep from bolting out of the restaurant.

"Are you always this reluctant to accept help from anyone?" My eyes follow as David takes a long draw off his glass of beer. Heat rises in my cheeks when I realize how badly I want to reach for him and lick the foam from his upper lip. "I'm offering you a reliable means of transportation so you won't have to waste your time and money on the bus."

"I know, I just—" I just what? Can't rely on anyone else? Don't want to spend time with him in a confined area because he makes my heart race and my palms sweat? Would be mortified for him to somehow find out that I live on the streets? There's no good explanation for why he can't give me a ride that won't in one way or another embarrass me. "I've gotta go."

My chair nearly topples to the floor in my haste to get out of this increasingly uncomfortable situation. I jerk away when David reaches for me. I can't talk to him right now. My stomach churns as I realize there's a good chance Bill will rescind his offer of permanent employment because I can't get along with David. I must have really fucked someone over in a past life because karma keeps reaching out to bite me square in the ass.

I run out of the restaurant, needing to get some air before I throw up all over. Somehow, it seems that would be a fitting end to my craptastic evening. It's not that far from the restaurant to downtown, so I decide to walk it instead of waiting on the bus. Yes, I have some money in my pocket right now because of pawning my phone, but I need to save every chance I get. David was right; taking the bus is going to get expensive when you add up two dollars to get there and two to get home every night. That's twenty dollars every week spent on transportation.

Lightning flashes in the distance and I quicken my pace. Just once, it would be fucking awesome to not be caught when these storms pop up.

Casey and Bree are nowhere to be found when I get back to the spot where we've hung out every night. The streets are quieter now than they were last week, but it seems those who are out partying tonight got an early start. No one stops to apologize for running into me, but they probably think I'm the one in the wrong as I stand in the middle of the sidewalk with my arms limp at my sides. I'm invisible. And once again, I'm alone.

I thought about excusing myself when Austin left the restaurant, but I stayed at the table to avoid raising any suspicions. Austin didn't simply leave, he bolted the way only fear can motivate a man to run. The moment I step onto the sidewalk, I wish I hadn't been so aware of his fears and discomfort. The rain is coming down in sheets as lightning brightens the night sky like strobe lights at a house party. As I make a mad dash to my own car, I wonder where Austin is now and if he's safe.

There's no peace to be had once I'm back to my hotel

room. I lay in the dark, still thinking about the young man with an unruly mop of brown waves and dull hazel eyes. I toss and turn in my bed, worrying that the rain will continue through the night and I won't see him tomorrow. Even worse, the thought pops into my head that even if the storms cease, my aggressiveness tonight may cause Austin to feel uncomfortable returning to the house tomorrow. I push those thoughts out of my head because the notion that he would forego a job opportunity he was eager to accept because of my advances is ludicrous.

On the drive to the house Sunday morning, I pull out my phone to call Chad and inform him of my plans to oversee the construction of my house. While it is unlikely he would allow most clients to get away with such behavior, I'm not most clients. I can only hope that will count for something and he won't ask me why I want to do this.

"You'd better have a good reason for calling so early," Chad groans when he answers. I glance down at the display on my dashboard and notice that it's not even eight in the morning. I pull into the parking lot of a coffee shop, figuring I might as well stop in and pick up donuts for the crew since they won't even be there for another hour yet. "Hey, you there?"

The terse tone in Chad's voice stops my mind from wandering too far down the path it's been on most of the night. "Sorry, I didn't realize it was so early. But yes, I do have a good reason."

Without giving Chad a chance to respond to anything I'm saying, I present my argument for why it will be beneficial to all involved for me to spend my summer playing construction worker. He grunts a few times, but otherwise gives me no indication of what he thinks of this proposal. Even when I stop talking, the other end of the line remains silent. "Did I lose you?" I ask, pulling the phone away from my ear to verify the call is still connected.

"No, I'm here. But I'm obviously not awake because I swear I just heard you say that you're going to help build your house. Have you even picked up a hammer since we were kids?" Chad chuckles at his own barb while I do not.

I understand where he's coming from; I have spent the better part of my adult life trying to distance myself from what can't even be considered humble beginnings. My family was so impoverished we made dirt poor look like the middle class and my primary goal in life has been to put as much distance between myself and my roots as possible. That means I take pride in the countless hours spent getting perfect grades throughout college, the recommendations my professors gave me that helped me secure my first teaching position, and now the fact that I have finally landed my dream job. Manual labor is something I didn't realize I enjoyed until given the opportunity.

"I'll have you know that I spent all day yesterday working with the crew," I say, feigning offense. "You can call Bill if you don't believe me and I'm sure he will give you a glowing recommendation."

"If you work half as hard as you did the year before college, there's no question about your work ethic. I guess I'm confused as to why you'd want to sweat your ass off all summer instead of relaxing before you start teaching." I consider reminding Chad that my "home" right now is a hotel room, which doesn't afford the room or quiet necessary to relax.

"It will get me outside and it beats spending time in the gym to combat the effects of working a fairly sedentary job. Plus, the more people working on my house, the sooner I can move in, so it's only fitting that I step up to the plate." *And, with any luck, it will allow me to get to know Austin a bit better.*

Yes, I am aware that my fascination with the much younger man is bordering on obsession. I spent more hours of my night than I would care to admit telling myself to let it go, to let *him* go, but I can't. The kid's in so much pain that it's nearly a tangible force following him around. Sure, he tries to hide it, but it isn't the type of burden that is easily hidden from those who have felt a similar weight on their soul. And dammit, I want to be the one to ease that burden, to show Austin that life will get better.

"I don't s'pose there's a problem with that. But are you sure it's how you want to spend your summer vacation?" Chad's baby girl coos into the phone and his attention fades to the little beauty in his arms. Being perpetually single, it's easy for me to forget that not everyone keeps the hours I do or has the freedoms I have.

"I'm sure I will still be able to get in some relaxation, but knowing what is happening at the house will go a long way to reducing my stress." I step out of my car and regret wearing long pants as the rain from last night is already boosting the morning humidity. "Why don't you go spend some time with your girls and give me a call later? There's something else I want to run past you, but it will take longer than I want to pull you away from your family this morning."

"Everything okay?" Chad asks.

"Yes, everything is fine. It's not anything about me, but I am hoping you will be able to help someone. He is a good kid, but needs a bit of stability in his life." Already, I feel as if I've said too much. For all I know, Bill may have talked to Chad before approaching Austin last night and my meddling could jeopardize his of-fer. "You know, forget I said anything," I quickly add, trying to salvage the conversation and wishing I had ended this call about a minute ago.

"Don't do that shit," Chad criticizes. "I want to hear more about this guy, but not right now. If I don't get Avery her breakfast, she's likely to eat my phone. Come by the house tonight for dinner and you can tell me all about him."

We end the call and I open the door to the coffee shop, grateful when I'm blasted by the almost uncomfortably cool air conditioning. While I'm there, I pick up sandwiches for myself and Austin on the off chance that I haven't scared him off.

Chapter Four

Austin

I f circumstances were different, I would have avoided Casey last night. The second I got back to the park, he knew something was wrong. I'm not sure how since we've only known one another for a short time, but he did. Maybe I just suck at pretending I'm okay when I'm not. The problem is, I'm not about to tell him *why* I was upset. The last time I let down my guard, I was shunned by the people who were supposed to love me no matter what; there's no way I can be that vulnerable out here.

"Dude, what's your problem? Ever since you let that pompous ass convince you to go to dinner, you've been acting weird."

Unfortunately, my options at this point are continued avoidance, which would mean missing out on the day of work, and likely having Bill take back the job offer, or suck it up and deal with Casey's inquest. The latter will suck less in the long run.

"Nothing. It was a long day and walking back in the rain sucked ass. Can you please just let it go?" I plead with him, staring out the window. It dawns on me as we drive through town that I've lived here for almost a year and have rarely ventured off campus. And this morning I'm captivated by the smallest details because it keeps me from having to open up to Casey.

"Whatever you say, man." Casey leans back in his seat. His silence is worse than his prying because now I'm sitting here freaking out that I've effectively alienated the one person who's been there for me recently.

The walk from the bus stop to the construction site brings more stony silence. I fucking hate this shit. I hate feeling like I'm walking around on eggshells because I've become reliant on the help of others to survive from day to day. I hate not having anyone to talk to when I'm freaking out because that leaves all that shit floating around in my head and my problems seem bigger than they are.

Casey steps in front of me just before we head up the gravel driveway. "Look, sorry about getting in your shit," he apologizes. I shield my eyes from the glare of the sun and see that he truly does seem remorseful for pushing so hard. "I just don't want people fucking with ya. You're a good guy when you're not being a little punk."

I duck away when he reaches up and ruffles my hair. It's odd, but I've also learned that the crew at the park relies on one another for simple affection. For some of them, it's a comfort they never had before hitting the streets. Still, I fucking hate it when people mess with my hair. It's the type of thing my family used to do and it makes me feel like whoever does it is talking down to me. There I go again, comparing the people in my life now to everyone in the past. It's a bad habit I really need to break.

"No worries," I assure him. "Sorry for being a little bitch. I'm still trying to navigate all this new life shit and it's been a long time since anyone asked what was going on and gave a damn to hear the answer."

Bill calls out to us before I can go any further, and I'm grateful for the interruption. Just because I see that what I'm doing is wrong doesn't mean I'm ready to dump all my shit on Casey's shoulders. I breathe a sigh of relief when I don't see David's car anywhere in the area and figure he's taking the day off. It wouldn't surprise me since he's not getting paid anything to be here.

Bill doesn't waste any time dividing out the work crew into teams. Most of the crew is working on the roof today, with the rest of us, the ones probably not covered under any sort of worker's comp insurance, are working on cleaning up the inside of the house. Ryan, our team leader, bitches non-stop about how pointless it is that we're even here since we're at a standstill until the electricians and plumbers come in to do their work. I don't care one way or the other, as long as there's an envelope of cash waiting for me at the end of the day.

Just when I think it's going to be a nice, easy, re-laxing day, I hear the velvety smooth voice that kept replaying in my mind all night, making sleep nearly impossible. "It looks great in here," David praises as he walks through each framed out room. I envy the way his chest puffs out with pride as he realizes how close his dream is to becoming a reality. And a part of me is proud for him because he told me on the way to dinner last night how long he's been saving up for this day.

"Oh, David, I didn't see you pull up," Bill says, stepping through a doorway. "I know you're eager to get caught up, but it's going to be an early day today because there's not much for most of the boys to do. Had I been on the ball yesterday, I would have told you not to bother coming down today."

"It's okay. I brought some baked goods and coffee for everyone. It's all set up on a couple of sawhorses in the garage." My stomach rumbles at the mention of food. I have enough left from pawning my phone that I could have grabbed something to eat this morning, but I'm trying to get used to eating less because I don't want to waste a single penny this summer. "Since we are ahead of schedule, would it be possible to speak with you for a moment?"

Maybe I'm seeing shit, but I swear David glances at me as he makes the request of Bill. The two of them huddle in the corner and I try to pay attention to what I'm supposed to be doing. By the time they're done talking, I haven't moved from my spot, but I've swept the same spot for so long that I swear the subfloor is going to have a groove from me brushing away a thin layer of wood particles.

David pats Bill on the shoulder and walks directly toward me. I pretend that I don't notice him as I move to the next pile of debris, which becomes more difficult when I can feel him standing over me, watching every move I make.

"Can you join me in the garage?" David asks, but I don't feel like it's much of a request. This is *his* house and if I say no, I can't guarantee that I will have the job Bill's been hinting at giving me. Working construction, while hot and miserable, will pay substantially more than a fast food joint or a retail store, so I need to keep Bill happy. I need the work if I have any hope of going to school in the fall.

"Yes, sir," I respond. I brush the dust off my jeans as I follow him. He turns his head to make sure I haven't bolted and flashes me a smile that could bring just about anyone to their knees. Everything about this man is polished. If not for the passion I saw in his eyes when he talked about how excited he is about this house, I would think he's too perfect. His speech, his mannerisms, even his wardrobe all scream pretentious. He is everything I want to get away from in my life, but with David, I feel like there's a hidden layer that explains why he is the way he is.

Everyone rushes out of the garage as David motions for me to get something to eat. I reach for a healthy looking muffin even though I really want the donut with chocolate frosting and sprinkles. It's about as moist as the sawdust I've spent the past hour sweeping into piles, but it's the responsible choice. It will give me more energy and keep me full longer, which is more important than having a tasty treat.

David overturns two buckets and sits on one of them. I cautiously follow suit and sit on the other. "Were you serious last night when you told Bill that you were interested in working for him this summer?" David asks.

"Yes, sir," I respond, wondering why he's asking me this. It's not like it matters to him, but the way he leans in as he talks to me, I start to feel like he truly cares.

"Austin, you don't have to call me sir. I'm just David, okay?" I nod and find a spot on the floor to hold my attention because I'm terrified to look into his eyes. He's too close, too friendly, and already he makes me want things I shouldn't with him. "Good. Now, I want you to come to dinner with me tonight."

I stand so quickly that I kick the bucket out from behind me. Everything I've been thinking about David is obviously way the fuck off base because now he's trying to bribe me. Fuck that. I storm down the driveway, ready to give up the only opportunity I've had to save myself because I'm not going to let anyone play games with me. Before I make it halfway to the street, David's hand is wrapped around my arm, pulling me back.

The urge to spin around and deliver a jab to his chiseled jaw is somewhere just below the surface. I clench my eyes closed, taking a few breaths as I remind myself there's no one to bail me out of jail if I do hit him and he presses charges.

"Get. Your hands. Off of me." Rather than listen to my demand, David's grip tightens when I try to jerk away from him. Now, I'm pissed. I turn on my heel and shove David away. "I don't know what fucked up game you're playing, but I'm not about to be your little bitch boy. If me working for Bill depends on me being at your beck and call, tell Bill I'll find something else. I'm *not a whore.*"

David stuffs his hands in the pockets of his oh-so-sexy, perfectly distressed jeans. And the arrogant fuck looks as if he's about to laugh at me.

"Is that what you truly believe I am trying to do?" David asks. I swallow hard, regretting saying anything. No, I don't really think David's trying to buy me, but no other scenario makes any sense. "Austin, look at me."

The tip of his finger crooks beneath my chin, forcing me to lift my gaze. What I see terrifies me more than the thought of trading my body for a job. David seems genuinely hurt by my accusation. Rather than apologize, I walk away. I'm not running this time, but I have to get someplace where I can sit before my knees buckle beneath me.

I sit on a boulder beside the house and David pushes me over as he settles back as well. "Austin, what is this about? Have I done something to offend you or make you feel uncomfortable?"

Has he? No. Yes. Fuck, I don't know anymore. If I sit back and really think about it, he's been nothing but kind to me. "No. Don't mind me, it's been a rough month and I'm a bit stressed." I chew at the inside of my lip to stop myself from saying anything else. David can't know why I'm stressed. Yes, I'm ashamed of my life as it is right now, but if no one else knows, I don't have to see the pity in their eyes.

"I do mind you, Austin." David places his hand on my knee, watching to see if I'm going to freak out again. I'm not. His hand feels good, like I'm somehow absorbing positive energy or some shit from him. I laugh at that thought because I never would have considered any of that new age bullshit until I started staying by Bree. She's the queen of positive thinking and says we'd all be better off if we weren't such downers all the time.

"Why?"

"Because I see a lot of myself in you," David admits. The man's apparently insane because we're nothing alike. I might have been like him when my entire life was an empty shell, crafted so we looked like the perfect family to all of my father's business associates.

Apparently, I do a shit job hiding my disbelief. "Don't look at me that way. I don't want to bore you with the details, but I will tell you that I have spent almost twenty years trying to evolve into the man I am today. It isn't easy and you have to be driven to succeed. When I look at you, I don't get the impression that you are a quitter, and I can see the fire in your eyes that says you know what you need to do and you will do anything to accomplish that goal. Your life is tough right now, you're likely living paycheck to paycheck, but you know that's not the end of your story."

I'm still skeptical that a man who drives around in a brand new Mazda Miata understands what my life is like, but it seems he's pretty much pegged where I am and what I feel. Well, except that whole paycheck thing. And he probably wouldn't guess where I live or how that whole situation came to be, but I'm not about to correct him. I want to push David to tell me more about how he overcame whatever it is he thought was pulling him under, but if I do, I know he'll want to know more about my story and I'm not ready to share that. I don't know that I ever will to anyone other than my friends at the park.

"Okay, so why me?" I ask. He could just as easily be offering to buy Casey dinner and help him find a job, but he's not. Just as Casey could have invited anyone to come out here for the weekend, but he asked me. What makes me so special that people want to help me? Do I give off some sort of helpless, pathetic vibes that everyone wants to do their part to save me?

"As I have already told you, you are the one who seems determined to change his circumstances without asking for help. I think you are scared that you will be perceived as weak because you should be someone other than you are today." I move away, uncomfortable with how close David is to my truth. I swear, if the man digs any deeper and gets any more details right, I'm going to freak the fuck out again.

"You may not know this, but Bill's boss is a good friend of mine from when I was a bit younger than you are. I am having dinner with him tonight and I would like for you to join us."

"Okay." My mind is shutting down now because David has my head running in so many different directions. I feel like a complete fool because now I see that he's not trying to flirt with me or get me into his bed, he's just a good guy. And I'm an idiot.

David

By mid-afternoon, there's no work left to be done today. That is fine by me because I want to get somewhere cool and quiet so I can learn more about Austin. The problem is that I can't invite him to hang out at my place because I'm not about to ask him to follow me to a hotel room, but I also don't feel comfortable inviting myself to his home. This leaves us at an impasse because I have no idea what to suggest we do for the few hours we have to spare before dinner with Chad.

"Uh, David?" I turn to see Austin once again staring at the ground. Something has happened in this young man's past to make him incredibly insecure.

"Yes, Austin?" I respond, wishing I could wrap my arms around him and get him to see my perception of what lies beneath his fragile exterior.

"So, I have to hurry if I'm going to make the bus but I was wondering where to meet you later."

This surprise me, but I feel a bit lighter knowing that he's not going to try to get out of tonight. Of course, he thinks I have asked him to join me because it will give him a chance to meet his future boss, but that's the way it has to be for now. Until I have a better read on him, I will do everything in my power to keep from making him uncomfortable.

"Would you like me to pick you up at your place?" I offer. I know Austin doesn't have a car and I have no clue where the buses run in this town. Besides, it would be impolite for me to invite him to dinner and then expect him to find his own way there.

Austin rubs at the back of his neck as he worries his lip between his teeth. I don't understand why, but he is once again allowing his nerves and insecurity to show.

"Uh, that's not as easy as it sounds," he says so quietly I barely hear him. "See, I live down on State Street and my place is in the middle of the block, so you'd have to park and then walk. Why don't we pick a place that'll be easier for you to get to and we'll meet there."

Every word seems to come quicker than the one before. It's as if he had to formulate what he wanted to say and then get it all out before I could see through the lie. And he's definitely lying to me because he won't look at me. Dishonesty is something I won't stand for in any circumstances, but I find myself allowing it from Austin. I dismiss his excuse on the assumption that he is trying to be polite and not tell me that he is uncomfortable with me knowing where he lives. In all actuality, it is smart for him to be cautious because we barely know one another.

"I am still fairly new to town, so you will have to tell me where you want to meet." By placing the decision in his hands, I hope he will begin to see that I don't wish to keep pushing him outside his comfort zone.

"Uh, do you know where the Union is?" He finally looks up at me and I see a light in his eyes that hasn't been there until now. It's a confidence that he wears well.

"Yes, that is one of the first places Chad insisted

we go when I first arrived. I will meet you there at five-thirty." It's amusing that he chose that location because it has quickly become the place I go whenever I want to be around people but not feel the need to engage in conversation. I can simply sit in one of the kitschy chairs and stare out at the lake.

"Okay, I really gotta hurry or I'll miss the bus." Austin waves back at me as he jogs down the street. We seem to have turned one corner on a very dangerous, winding path.

Chapter Five

Austin

I feel disgusting. Summers suck enough, but with nowhere to shower, it's nearly unbearable. And I have to find a way to get cleaned up because I don't want to smell like I've spent a week living in a dumpster when I walk into dinner with David. As much as I hate to part with my money, I head to Walgreens to pick up a few things to help me look presentable.

When I get back, I ask Bree what she suggests doing. When I tell her that David invited me to dinner, the girl practically bounces as she squeals in delight. She seems more excited than I am, but she also isn't the one who has to find a way to not seem so out of place.

Bree tugs on my hand and the next thing I know we're practically running up the sidewalk, against the flow of foot traffic, until suddenly we're not. She stops without warning, causing me to crash into her back and we both fall to the ground. As I block out the snide comments of an uptight soccer mom, I realize that *this* is what I've been missing. I've been so caught up in the bullshit that is my life lately that I can't remember the last time I laughed uncontrollably or did anything remotely crazy.

As I pull Bree off the sidewalk, I pull her in and kiss her cheek. "Thank you," I say quietly.

"I haven't done anything, yet," she responds, one pierced eyebrow quirked in confusion.

"Yes, you have. But if I explain it to you, I'm afraid this feeling will go away and it's nice to not feel as if I'm being crushed by my own drama for once," I admit. Bree doesn't say anything, she knows there's nothing more to be said. She leads me through the door and up a steep, dark staircase. At the top landing, she digs into the bottom of her patchwork bag, coming out with a key on an old plastic keychain.

With the flick of her wrist, we're inside a cute, girly studio apartment. One wall is lined with pencil and chalk drawings, much like the ones Bree creates every night on the street. And sitting on the end of the couch is my backpack and duffel bag. How in the—

"Bree, where are we?" I ask, taking a step further into the apartment to verify that yes, those are indeed my bags where they very much don't belong.

Without responding, Bree opens a window along the front wall, allowing a warm breeze to cut through the stagnant air. Next, she makes her way to a small cabinet, pulling out a towel and washcloth.

"Austin, please don't tell Casey that I brought you here." She looks like a kid who just got caught doing something wrong. What I can't figure out is *why* she feels that way. She has a key to this place and knows her way around, so it's obvious she's allowed to be here.

"Um, sure," I acquiesce, still oblivious to why it would be such a bad thing. Maybe I should ask, but my mind is stuck on the fact that Bree is handing me a soft towel and directing me into a bathroom with running water. The last time I took a real shower was over a week ago, which isn't as bad as it sounds, thanks to Casey and Bree showing me the ropes when it comes to the basics of life. That thought snaps me back to the lunacy of this situation. "Care to fill me in on why he'd be upset that I'm here? And again, what is this place?"

"After your shower. You don't have a ton of time." She shoos me away as she picks up—a laptop?—from the coffee table. The only thing getting her off the hook is the fact that she's right and I need to get going.

As soon as I step out of the shower, I realize I've screwed up. "Bree, can you grab me some clothes out of my bag?" I feel bad asking her, but the other option is for me to walk out in nothing but a towel, which would both embarrass me and likely piss off Casey.

A handful of clothes appear almost instantly around the edge of the door, which I've cracked open to release some of the steam. "It's good that only one of us is freaking about your date with tall, dark and handsome," she teases.

"It's not a date," I remind her again. "He's just a good guy and wants me to meet with the owner of the construction company."

"Would that make him a sugar daddy?" Bree presses. "Because, you know, there's nothing wrong with a sexy older man who wants to take care of you."

"First, I'm pretty sure a sugar daddy would be paying for everything for me, not helping me find a job," I point out. "And second, how do you know he's older?"

That's one detail I didn't mention to her because it doesn't matter. Sure, it might be an issue if I was looking for a love connection, but I'm not. Not at all.

"Casey told me how the guy kept making eyes at you yesterday. Don't worry, it's cool if you're gay," she quickly adds. "Actually, you'd be surprised how many people sleeping in the park every night are there because their parents kicked them to the curb when they came out. It's sad, really."

"Why are you there?" I ask, still waiting impatiently for her to clue me in on why she's supposedly homeless, but we're in an apartment that feels an awful lot like home.

"Casey."

"Huh?" I mutter around my toothbrush. As I finish getting ready, Bree tells me all about how she and Casey met. He's homeless by circumstance; she's there because she loves him.

"That makes no sense to me. You have this killer apartment, not to mention a bed, bathroom and everything else, and yet you *choose* to sleep on concrete?" I realize how judgmental I sound, but seriously, it's borderline insanity. "Why don't the two of you live here together?"

"Because Casey has a penis," she deadpans. When I don't respond, she elaborates after an exaggerated sigh. "When I asked him to move in with me, he got all shitty about it. He doesn't want me to resent him for having to be his savior, or some equally stupid shit. So, I packed up a bag and headed down to stay with him."

"But won't you resent him anyway since you've given up everything to be with him?" I check the clock and see I have about twenty minutes before I have to meet David. That means I have less than ten to solve the riddle that is Bree and Casey.

"Nah, this is all just stuff." She says that, but I don't miss the way she pets her laptop as she says the words. She misses her stuff. "And he knows that I come here when he's off working. Hopefully, he'll land something solid soon and then it won't be an issue. Then, he can afford to pay his half of the rent, we can sleep in the bed and not have to deal with smelling like a dumpster half the time."

The longer Bree speaks, the less appealing being homeless for any length of time sounds. Not that it's some romantic notion to live like a pauper, never knowing where the next meal is going to come from, but so far it hasn't been that bad. About the time I start hoping that Casey finds something soon so he can save his relationship, guilt creeps into my mind. He's the one who got me the job for the weekend, but I'm the one walking away with a possible permanent job.

"Bree, Casey's not pissed at me because of Bill's offer, is he?" He hasn't acted as if he's upset, but I know I would be if I were in his shoes. This job should have gone to him, not me.

"Hell no! That's part of what pisses me off about him. He knows I don't like the way we live, but he knows I'm not going to leave him out there while I sleep alone. It sucks," she whines, flopping back onto the couch next to me. "Sometimes, I think he's waiting for me to get sick of him, and he figures it's easier this way because then he won't have to get used to having a home just to have it yanked out from under him again."

I realize now that this is the most she's shared with me about their situation. Before now, I assumed they lived together and lost their home. This is the exact opposite and even more confusing. A million questions flood my mind, but there's no time for that now. I need to get to the union before David thinks I'm flaking on him.

Bree pushes my hand away when I try to grab my bags. I'm not sure what I'm going to do with them, but I can't leave them here. I also can't expect her to babysit my shit while I'm chillin' with people about twenty rings higher on the food chain.

"I'll deal with that so you don't get dirty or sweaty. The whole reason we came up here was so you could look decent." When I try to argue with her, she pinches my cheeks so I can't speak. "Trust me, Austin. This is what we do for one another up here."

I lean in to kiss Bree's cheek, thanking whatever force brought her into my life. "You rock. If Casey doesn't get his shit together, let me know, and I might have to kick his ass and switch teams so I can show the boy how to treat a woman."

Bree lets out a breathy giggle. "Thanks, but I don't really see any of that happening. He'd snap you like a twig and I've seen the way you look at the guys when you think no one is watching. I'm pretty sure there's not a single bone in your body that could be attracted to a girl; even one as awesome as me."

We both laugh all the way down the stairs. And she's right, the times I've tried dating girls just to appease my parents were some of the most miserable months of my life. Everything about them felt wrong to me. They were too soft, smelled too sweet and kissed the way they had seen couples kiss in cheesy romantic comedies. I wanted someone hard, spicy and who would kiss me as if they were starving and I was a slab of prime rib, or at least a juicy bar burger. If people like that existed in east central Minnesota, I never saw any of them. I'm pretty sure they're there, but more than likely as deep in their own closets as I was until I got a taste of freedom.

I expect Bree to say goodbye as we reach the park, but she yells out to Casey that she'll be right back. "You've got to be out of your mind if you think I'm not going to see if this guy is as hot as Casey made him out to be."

"Wait, Casey said he's hot?" Casey seems like the last person who would mention the stubble accentuating David's jaw or the way his eyes sparkle when he laughs. Shit, that sounds gay even to my ears.

"No, Casey said he's good looking, which means he's hot." I cock my head to the side, wonder what the difference is in her mind, or at least how the two vary in Casey's mind. "Look, in case you didn't realize it, Casey's pretty careful about making sure everyone knows that he's not into guys. I mean, he's not an asshole about gays, but he had a few guys who were assholes when he first got out here. One kid mistook Casey being nice for Casey wanting to screw him and another thought that he could turn a no into a yes if he was persistent enough."

I don't know what to say to that. Part of me wants to apologize, but that's just stupid because it's not like I was the jackass in either of those situations. My default reaction would be to make some sort of a smartass comment, but that seems equally inappropriate, so I say nothing.

About the time that the awkward silence becomes too much to handle, I look up and am rewarded by a stunning sight; David leaning against the side of his car, wearing khaki shorts and a light blue button-down shirt with the sleeves rolled up. The top two buttons of the shirt are open, giving me the slightest hint of nearly black chest hair. It doesn't seem to be thick, just enough to make my fingers twitch with the need to know what it would feel like against my skin.

David looks up from his cell phone as I approach and flashes a brilliant smile. Bree gasps next to me. "Good lord, if you don't do that man I'm going to be very disappointed in you," she teases.

"Shut up," I mutter, trying to play it cool. The last thing I need is David thinking that I've made him out to be a love interest to my friends. "Hey, David!"

My breath is stolen from me as David pushes off the car and drapes one arm over my shoulder. It's a casual move, but in my over-active mind, it's an invitation to so much more. I have to fight the urge to lean into him and bury my face against his chest. Although I've accepted my sexuality for a long time and vowed to live my life for me the night I came out to my family, David is the first person who's made me *want* to do more than fantasize.

"Austin, it's good to see you." He looks down at my outfit, a simple white t-shirt and jeans paired with the one pair of shoes I own, and I feel incredibly under-dressed. "You look great."

I look up at him to see if he's being sarcastic. What I see staring down at me is the same guarded interest I feel for him. I can't bring myself to come right out and ask if the man is gay, but dammit, I fully intend to find out before the night is through. Otherwise, I'm going to drive myself crazy with this back and forth.

"Thanks." I look over my shoulder and see Bree watching the entire exchange, a knowing smile on her face. David notices her about that time and I wonder how I should explain her presence.

"Hi, I'm Bree," she says, holding out her hand to David. David takes her proffered hand and introduces himself as well. "Austin, have a good time. Remember what I told you."

She kisses my cheek and takes off up the street. Whether she realized it or not, she was my safety net and now I have none. It's a daunting thought, one that threatens to pull me back into the darkness of my mind.

Like a true gentleman, David opens the car door for me before walking around to the driver's side. On the way to his friend's house, he tells me that they met when they both took a year off between high school and college to work for some sort of service organization. I never even knew shit like that existed, but it sounds pretty cool as he tells me about the work they did. By the time we pull up in front of a home magnificent enough to make my mother jealous, I'm no longer anxious about the evening.

Austin seems more relaxed than he was when I picked him up, but I can tell he is still uncomfortable. I can't say I blame him since he doesn't know any of us all that well and he is by far the youngest adult in the room, but I want to find a way to pull him out of his shell.

Throughout dinner, I watch him carefully for any sign that he wants to leave. And then I chastise myself for how upset that idea makes me. Saying it feels good to have him here, with the friends who have become more like family to me over the years, is an understatement. There is a voice deep in my head telling me that it's not only nice, but this is how it is supposed to be. He belongs here at the table with the rest of us.

Now, I simply have to make him believe as much.

Chad pulls me out to the back yard after we are through eating. I assume we are going to talk about Austin and whether or not Chad thinks he has a job for him, but Chad's furrowed brow is the first indication that there is something else he hopes to talk about.

"You can't save him," Chad says flatly as he turns to walk away from me. "I know you and I can see that look on your face that says you think it's your job, but it's not. And if you try, you're going to fuck it all up."

"I'm not sure what you mean," I respond. Chad motions for me to sit in the chair next to him, pulling two beers out of a cooler when I do. "I'm not trying to save him, I just—"

"You just want to help him," Chad finishes for me. "Look, we've been friends for a long time so don't try to bullshit me. The kid's got skeletons, that's for damn sure, but you can't sweep them away for him. I saw the way you look at him; it's almost sickening how you get this goofy look on your face every time he comes into view. And that's what worries me."

"I promise, I'm not trying to rescue the kid," I reiterate. "He needs a job, you need help and I have seen how hard he works. That's as far as my involvement goes."

Neither of us say anything after that little lie. Even I don't believe that I will be satisfied with nothing more than helping Austin land a good paying job for the summer. If that were my intention, I wouldn't have had to do anything because Bill had already offered him work.

Austin and Chad's wife join us around the pool a short time later. The two of them seem to be getting along quite well, which pleases me. I want him to feel the same sense of belonging and peace I feel and it doesn't take much to realize he doesn't feel that often. Even earlier, when his friend walked with him to meet me, he was guarded. But now, that wall is down and the two of them are laughing as if they've known one another for years. In the soft lights around the perimeter of the deck, I can see the way his eyes shine with mirth. It is truly a breathtaking sight.

We stay late into the night and Chad finally relaxes after speaking with Austin about what each of them are looking for in terms of the job. Hopefully, that means he has come to realize that Austin isn't a pile of broken glass that needs to be pieced back together, but more a rare treasure that needs to be cared for. I look to the side table after that flowery thought and realize I've had entirely too much to drink tonight. In contrast, Austin has been nursing the same can of soda for over an hour.

My irresponsibility leaves three options, none of which are good; we can both stay at Chad's for the night since I'm not about to drive, otherwise I have to see if Austin knows how to drive a manual and he can either drive us to my hotel or his apartment. I could also have him drop me off and I could call him a cab, but I'm not ready for the night to end. Now that the ice has thawed a bit between us, I want to spend some time alone with Austin to find out where his head is at.

I call him over to me when Chad disappears into the house. Much to my surprise and pleasure, Austin is no longer skittish in my presence. He sits next to me on the chaise and I have to suck in a sharp breath to get my libido under control. I slide over, both to give him more room and to give myself some space so I'm not feeling his tight backside pressing against my leg.

"I believe it's about time we should let Chad and Becky get to sleep," I inform him. Austin's shoulders slump at my words. I should feel like a bastard for how much his disappointment pleases me, but I don't. I place my hand on his leg, squeezing gently until he looks at me. "The problem is that I seem to have lost count of how many drinks Chad passed me. Now, they do have a guest bedroom, which you could use and I could sleep on the couch, but I don't want you to feel uncomfortable.

"I also fear that you'll be just as uneasy about the solutions I've come up with for this predicament I seem to have gotten us into." My thumb traces circles over the soft denim of Austin's pants and he begins to fidget. I lift my hand, but he quickly catches it in his own, placing our joined hands on his thigh.

"What's that?" Austin's voice cracks.

"Do you know how to drive a stick?" Austin nods. "Then I would like for us to say goodnight and head back to my place. As you know, I don't have a house yet, so it is a hotel room, but I assure you this isn't some move to get you into bed. I want to spend some time without an audience so we can speak freely and get to know one another."

"But why?" I sit forward, no longer giving a damn about propriety because Austin needs to begin to understand his worth. Someone, at some point in the past, has made him feel as if he's disposable and that infuriates me. Of course, I could be dead wrong about that, but I don't believe that I am. It's obvious in the way he shakes his head in disbelief as he awaits my answer. The way his leg bounces nervously.

Austin doesn't pull away when I wrap my arms around his waist. No, the kid surprises me by leaning into my body and both of us fall back onto the cushion of the chair. He tries to get away, but this time I'm not letting him run. I tighten my grip and wait for his body to relax. He does and I tenderly kiss the top of his head.

It doesn't take long for me to realize what the alcohol has done to my resolve. I just told Austin I'm not trying to sleep with him and less than a minute later, the two of us are lying in a lover's embrace. I push myself so I'm sitting and lace my fingers with Austin's so he understands that I'm not rejecting him.

"Because I like you," I admit. It sounds like something a boy would say to someone in the fifth grade, but it's the truth. "And I would like to know more about you."

"You don't think I'm just some dumb kid?" he asks.

God no, I want to say. I want to tell him everything I see when I look at him but I don't think he's ready for that. "No," I say firmly. "You may be young, but you certainly aren't dumb."

"And it doesn't bother you that I'm so much younger than you?" he presses. It's as if he is hoping that I will see the error in my judgment if he offers enough potential issues.

"Do you even know how old I am?" I respond. We haven't discussed age because it isn't important to me. It never has been when it comes to friends or lovers. What matters is having a connection with the people I choose to have in my life and I've felt that with Austin since the moment I laid eyes on him. What I'm trying to figure out now is which category he will fall into.

"No, but—"

I cut him off before he can issue another self-deprecating statement or excuse as to why I shouldn't have an interest in anything more than a professional relationship with him. "Austin, I'm going to ask you one question and I want an honest answer. Can you do that for me?"

"Yes."

"Are you interested in getting to know me?" My heart races once the words leave my mouth.

Austin runs his hands through his hair, making the already unruly waves take on the appearance of having just gotten out of bed. Which makes me think about what he *would* look like first thing in the morning and I'm certain it would be a spectacular sight. His head bows to the ground and he mutters something so quietly I can't hear his response.

"I'm sorry, what was that?"

"Yes, but I didn't think—"

That's all I need to hear. I abruptly stand from the chair, almost knocking Austin to the ground. I take his hand and lead him back to the house so we can say goodnight to our hosts. Hopefully, this will be the first of many times the two of us are here.

"This is a bad idea," Chad whispers into my ear as he gives me a hug. What he fails to realize is that almost twenty years ago, he was the one doing the saving and I was in Austin's shoes. No, there was no romantic interest there, but I doubt either of us regret the help he gave me, the unconditional support he showed me. "Just be careful, okay?"

"Always," I promise him. "Thank you for everything." We both know that I'm not only talking about his helping Austin or anything else in our current lives. I'm thanking him for everything he's done over the years to push me to where I am in my life today.

Chapter Six

Austin

David takes my hand in his as soon as we're in the parking lot of his hotel. I can almost hear my father's voice ringing in my ears, telling me what a disgusting piece of shit I am for allowing a man I barely know to take me into a hotel room late at night. My stomach churns and I think about asking David to call a cab since the buses don't run this late. But that would require spending money I'm trying so hard to save, so I let him lead me through the lobby, down the hall to his first floor suite.

Not so long ago, I would have turned up my spoiled nose at such a simple room, but now it's a palace in my mind. While not luxurious by any stretch of the imagination, there is a full kitchen, a small living area with table and chairs, and a huge bed in a separate room. My mind wanders not only to what David could do to me in that bed, but what it would feel like to sleep on something that provides more comfort than a sleeping bag on concrete can provide.

"Would you like something to drink?" David offers. He pulls out two bottles of water without waiting for my answer and ushers me to the small couch. I suppose it would technically be called a loveseat by most people, but thinking that leads me to think about why it might have gotten that name and I'm not going down that road. I lean against one arm and David mirrors my posture on the other arm.

Now that we're here, it seems neither of us know what to say. He watches me sip from my bottle, crinkling the recycled plastic in my fingers. I used to be the guy who got the party started, the one everyone looked to when there was a lull, but sitting here with David, I feel out of my element as I never have before.

Everything about him screams success: the import sports car, the custom-built house, his designer clothes. All of these would be considered status symbols to most, but David doesn't strike me as the type of man to spend his money frivolously. The fact that he doesn't phased by such petty things is my undoing. It puts me in an uncomfortable position because I used to be the punk who *did* care about making sure everyone knew what new name-brand items I had convinced my parents to buy for me.

The more I take in the man sitting before me, the more I feel this was a huge mistake. We have no common ground, other than the fact that I'm helping build the house that he will someday live in, and I will go back to worrying about whether or not I will sleep so deeply that everything I own disappears due to my inattention.

"Austin, say something," David urges. He picks at his shorts despite the fact there's nothing on them and I relax a bit seeing that he's not much more comfortable than I am.

"What do you want me to say?" I turn my attention to the window, watching traffic sail by on the highway in the distance.

"Tell me something about yourself," he responds. His voice is kinder than I'm used to. For just a second, I allow myself to think this man might actually give a shit. That will surely change when he realizes how inexperienced I am. No, I don't think his interest is purely sexual, and yes, I am definitely interested in more than talking with him, but again, it comes down to crossing the line between theory and reality.

"Not really much to tell." *Because anything I say to you will be too much.*

"Everyone has a story, Austin." He leans forward, once again settling his hand on my knee. "I want to know yours, but if you're not ready or able to share, how about you ask me a question instead?"

That wasn't at all what I was expecting. I figured he'd be like the people in my past, pushing to know the minute details they had no right to so they could exploit them at their leisure. "Okay, how old are you?"

I roll my eyes because that sounds stupid to my ears. It's a question for the playground, not two grown men relaxing in a hotel room. "I'm thirty-five."

The fact that he's fifteen years older than I am doesn't bother me, it intrigues me. I wait for him to ask the same of me, but he doesn't and the silence returns.

"Where are you originally from?"

"Middle of nowhere in Kansas." David doesn't miss a beat sharing information about himself. This is a game, one where he shows his own willingness to share so I feel compelled to return the favor.

We continue like this for nearly an hour; me asking him the most basic, ridiculous questions I can while I try to avoid striking the nerve that will cause him to demand that I open up to him. David excuses himself to get more comfortable and as the door to the bedroom closes, my cock stirs thinking about what he looks like right now standing on the other side of the wall mostly naked.

When he returns, he turns out the overhead light, leaving only a small lamp on the side table to illuminate the room. "Come here," he says quietly, holding out a hand as he stands in front of me wearing cotton lounge pants and a t-shirt.

For reasons I can't explain, I take his hand, allowing him to pull me up so we're standing chest to chest. I look into his rich brown eyes and wonder if this is the moment I've dreamed of since I was thirteen years old and my best friend made out with a girl for the first time. The entire time he told me about feeling Katie Hammer's tits under her shirt, I was thinking about what it would be like to have strong arms wrapped around me, sliding my hands against his skin. But that was a secret I couldn't share with anyone, not even Jersey.

David's hands glide down my arms and around my waist. One hand stays and the small of my back while the other pulls my head to rest against his chest. I stand there, stiff in more ways than one, trying to figure out what to do. David misreads my unease and I feel his hold on my body loosen.

"No, don't," I beg. I feel like a little bitch, but I'm not ready for him to release me. I force my body to relax as I place my own hands on his hips. He might decide I'm not worth the effort, but he has to know the truth. "I've never done this before."

David leans back and looks down at me. "You've never done *what* before?" he asks, which makes me question the implication of my words. How far do I think this man is going to push me?

"Any of it," I whisper, burying my face in his chest to hide the flush of my cheeks. I've hugged people before, I've even kissed and made out, but not with someone who makes me hard with a single look. Not with someone I can be me around.

Without letting me go, David walks back to the couch, pulling me down to rest between his legs. "What do you *want* to do, Austin?"

Because it feels right, I lay on my side, breathing deeply to take in the way he smells. His fingers comb through my too-long hair but he doesn't rush me to answer. The part of me that realizes how much I've neglected my needs for my entire life wants everything, but mostly I'm scared. Somehow, simply laying with David makes the truth I've known forever that much more real. It's not a phase, as my father insists, it's who I am.

"I don't know," I finally admit.

"Is this too much?" I can practically hear the need in David's voice, the silent prayer that I won't tell him to stop. And right about now, that's the one thing I'm certain of; letting him hold me feels too good to even think of stopping. I shake my head, too overwhelmed by everything I'm feeling to say a word. "Then we'll stay like this."

David reaches behind his head for the remote and turns on the television. He flips through the channels, finally landing on a crime drama. There wasn't much time during second semester to watch anything unrelated to my studies, but this is a show I used to enjoy. As we both relax, I lift my hand to his chest and allow myself to just be. I don't worry about tomorrow, don't think about my family. Right now, it's just David and me and the glow of the television.

David

A s the credits roll, I look down to see Austin sound asleep on my chest. If possible, he seems even younger without the tense worry etched on his face. He looks, as I'm certain his is, innocent.

I push him forward slightly so I can get up from the couch. Perhaps the intelligent decision would be to leave him here for the night, but that's not going to happen. The way he melted in my arms, I wonder how long it has been since he's felt sincere affection from anyone in his life. I retreat to the bedroom, turning down the quilt and turning on one of the nightstand lamps before asking him to join me.

I won't lie and say the thought of having him in my bed doesn't excite me, but that's not what tonight is about. Tonight, I want to make sure Austin understands what it means to be cared for and adored without any expectations.

"Austin...honey, let's get you to bed," I whisper. When he doesn't stir, I crouch beside him, ghosting the back of my fingers against the smooth line of his jaw. His nose crinkles at the touch, but otherwise he remains still. "Come on, let's get more comfortable."

Austin's eyes crack open and he stares blankly in my direction. Suddenly, it dawns on him that he's not where he belongs and there's someone he's not used to mere inches from his beautiful face and his eyes grow wide. "What? Where?" he stammers, sitting so quickly he almost hits me. I fall back onto the floor, scooting as close as possible while trying to give him space to wake up.

"It's time for bed," I tell him. He shakes his head nervously. To ease his fears, I reach for his hands. "Austin, I'm not going to do anything with or to you tonight. The bed is big enough that both of us can sleep without even having to touch one another. If you sleep out here, you're going to be stiff in the morning."

Austin snorts, which gets me laughing. I have to remember that he's still young enough that anything I say can, and probably will, have double meaning. "I mean your back and neck will hurt, you little pervert," I tease, pulling him off the couch.

We stand in the darkness, not touching anywhere other than our hands, but Austin doesn't shy away this time. "You...you'd really be okay with just sleeping?" he asks.

"Yes," I promise him. I lead him to his side of the bed. He sits, wringing his hands and I kneel before him because he won't look at me. This way, he can't avoid seeing me, even with his eyes averted to the floor. "Austin, it's okay. I'm not sure what has happened to you in the past to make you question this, but my motives are pure, I can assure you." I pause for a moment, because that's not entirely true. "Okay, I will admit there are plenty of things I would love to do with you, but not tonight. For now, my only desire is to know you're able to sleep comfortably seeing as I all but forced you to come here."

"You didn't force me." Austin's hand slowly moves to the back of my neck. His grip is light and his fingers tremble slightly. "It's not that I don't want to be here. I do, I just..."

While Austin composes what he wants to say next, I reach down and begin untying his shoes. After pulling them off, I continue with his socks.

"What are you doing?" he asks. I look up in time to see his throat dip as he swallows hard. No matter what I say to Austin, it seems as if he is waiting for me to change my mind, to begin pressuring him to do what I want rather than what he needs.

"I'm taking off your socks and shoes," I say dryly. "Unless, of course, you thought you would sleep in them so you can bolt in the middle of the night." The words are meant to be a joke, but Austin winces.

"I...no..." He closes his eyes and when he opens them, we're back to square one. Austin is once again the unsure, insecure boy I met yesterday.

I take a seat next to him on the mattress, pushing on his shoulders so he's looking toward me. "Let me put this another way, Austin. It wouldn't matter to me if you were naked as the day you were born, I'm not going to do anything."

"God, you probably think I'm being ridiculous, don't you?" he huffs, burying his face in his hands. "I'm sorry, I just—"

To keep him from launching into a self-deprecating rant about his lack of experience, I lean forward, gently brushing my lips against his. He tenses, and then relaxes as I tightly grip his chin, holding him to me. It's one step beyond where I told him I would go tonight, but we both need this. Austin is tentative, but finally, I feel his jaw slacken as I press kisses across his cheek, creeping closer to his mouth.

"I'm going to kiss you," I warn him. My hand slides under his chin, holding him in place. Austin nods and I seal my mouth over his. The room is filled with gentle moans of pleasure as my tongue dips into his mouth. Just as I thought, innocent.

Before the moment can be ruined, I break the kiss.

I push him back on the bed and turn his body so his head is nestled by the pillows. Without trying to disrobe him, I pull the covers over his chest and lean down to give him a tender kiss on his forehead.

When I come back from the bathroom, I notice his shirt and jeans, neatly folded on the floor next to the bed. I smile, knowing that I have earned a bit of his trust and stifle a groan when I realize that I'm going to be sharing a bed with a nearly naked man and I can't do anything about it.

After turning out the light, I lie down on my side of the bed, maintaining an uncomfortable distance because I gave Austin my word. He's curled on his side, face pointing away from me. I could spend all night lying here, simply watching him sleep.

"My parents kicked me out when I told them that I'm gay." The admission startles me. "My dad was going on and on about how the queers are ruining the world and how they think everyone should cater to their disgusting wishes and I snapped one night. He bought me a bus ticket, reminding me that the car was in his name, and that was it. Said I could come back when I got over this phase."

Throwing my promise out the window, I scoot closer to Austin, pulling him into my arms. I hold him tight as he cries tears that he's held in for far too long. "Is that why you're trying to find a job?"

"Yeah," he sighs. "I want to prove to my father that I don't need him to support me. I don't want his help if he's really disgusted by who I am. What he doesn't get is that I'm the same kid I was before I came out, the only difference is that I won't be bringing a girl home ever again because I can't do that to myself or to them."

"What do you mean?" Perhaps it's unwise of me to

press him to say anything more, but now that he's comfortable, I want him to know he's also safe. Whatever he says to me is between us and he will never be judged or cast aside because of it.

"Didn't you ever date a girl because it's what you were supposed to do?" he asks. He pulls his arm out from inside my hold and runs his fingers along mine.

"Never." I wish all parents were like my own mother. When I told her I was gay, she simply kissed my cheek and asked me if I planned on telling her something she didn't already know. We were dirt poor, so there wasn't a long line of girls asking me to go out with them and I didn't have a broad circle of friends, so it was always the two of us sitting at home. I guess she put two and two together when it was the chiseled men with deep voices who captured my attention on the shows we would watch every night.

"Must be nice," Austin grumbles. "My parents expected me to be the all-American boy. Hell, it was bad enough that I played soccer instead of football, they never would have stood for me not showing an interest in the popular girls in my school."

I kiss Austin's bare shoulder when he goes quiet again, wishing I could learn everything, find out how he turned into the man he is today because he is none of that. Austin sighs heavily and I know sharing time is over for tonight.

"Get some sleep," I urge him. "Tomorrow, we can talk more over breakfast before I have to take you home."

"Thank you, David." Austin lifts my hand to his mouth for a tender kiss. His grip loosens after a few minutes and his breathing evens out as he falls asleep.

Chapter Seven

Austin

Every morning, I check my phone to see if there's a message from Bill or Chad, letting me know when I will be able to start work. It seemed like everything was turning around last weekend, but now it's been almost a week since I've heard from them. Chad told me Sunday night that he wouldn't have anything for me until after some of the other contractors had been in to do the more specialized work, but with every passing day, I lose faith that their words were anything more than empty promises.

"I swear, I'm about ready to throw that fucking thing in the lake," Casey groans when I take the phone out of my pocket for probably the twentieth time this morning. "Look, I know you thought shit was going to pan out, but it doesn't always work that way. And you said yourself that no one wants to take a chance on a kid with no experience and no stability in his life. It's just the way it is out here."

I'm not sure what's going on with him, but Casey seems to be on edge as well lately. The first week I was up here, he was this carefree drifter, not letting the world get him down, but now he's about as bitchy as a girl with PMS. The only difference that I know of is the fact that I had a job offer and he didn't.

"Are you pissed at me?" I ask, digging into my backpack for a bag of granola. "I told you I didn't ask them about work and I don't know why they made me an offer and not you. I know you and—"

Before I can say another word, Bree slaps me upside the back of my head. I cringe, realizing that I just about spewed a bunch of shit that Casey doesn't even realize I know. She and I have spent quite a bit of the week holed up in her apartment while Casey's been out trying to find a job. The more she tells me about my new friend, the more I don't understand him. I mean, I get that he has his pride, but what good will that do him if he can't support himself on the most basic levels?

"What do you think you know about me?" Casey growls. He leaps up from his seat and starts pacing up and down the hill, twisting his nappy dreads around his hand. "You think living out here for a couple of weeks makes you an expert? Let me tell you something...it doesn't mean dick. You won't get that until you hit your bottom. Sure, you think you're there now, but you're far from it. Bottom is when you can't even remember what it's like to sleep in a real bed, when you don't even wish for it because it won't happen. Bottom is when you don't feel the hunger pangs anymore because it's been so long since you had a full stomach.

"Bottom is the place you hit when no one even sees

you anymore. They don't take you seriously, no matter how much you try to prove yourself." Casey whips his hemp bag off the ground and storms away, leaving Bree and me to pick our jaws up off the ground.

Maybe he's right. Maybe neither of us understand where he's coming from. I refuse to believe that being without a roof over my head is anything more than a temporary setback and Bree is at war with herself because she *has* a home, but worries that staying there will create a chasm between herself and the man she loves. Too late.

Neither of us says anything as we walk to the apartment. After Casey's outburst, I feel like a fraud because he's right; I don't get what it's like to no longer have hope. And I cherish every fucking minute I get to spend sitting on a comfortable couch, using Bree's Wi-Fi to try to find solutions to the myriad roadblocks standing in my way.

Shortly after noon, my phone vibrates across the coffee table. I ignore it at first because I'm researching how to get around using my parents' income on my financial aid information. If I didn't have to count on their contribution, I would qualify for the aid I need to make staying in school a feasible option. By the fourth time the phone goes off, it's danced its way to the edge of the table so I pick it up to avoid watching it crash to the floor.

There's no hiding the smile when I see that all four messages are from David, asking if I have plans this weekend. It's the first I have heard from him since he dropped me off late Monday morning. It stung the first night because the memory of having him hold me was fresh in my mind. By Tuesday afternoon, I started to wonder if I had shared too much and scared him away. Wednesday, I blamed my evasiveness when he offered to walk with me to my (non-existent) apartment. Yesterday, I scolded myself anytime I started to think about what could have been.

I sit there staring at the phone, debating whether or not I'm a fool for feeling so damn giddy. After all, the few things I've allowed myself to look forward to seem to have evaporated, so why would David's interest in me be any different?

Me: No plans. What did you have in mind?

I can't help the butterflies dancing in my stomach as I hit send.

David: Nothing concrete, but I would like to spend time with you again. My bed has been cold without you.

"Oh, my God! I knew it!" Bree squeals, flopping over the back of the couch. I didn't even think to see if she was reading over my shoulder.

"Bree, you don't know shit," I respond. She poked and prodded for a while, trying to get me to spill every gory detail about my night with David. She went so far as to tell me it was my duty to tell her because she kept my shit safe while I was gone. It didn't work and she sulked away grumbling about what a shitty gay best friend I am if I wouldn't dish. Until then, I didn't realize I was any sort of best friend to her or anyone else. Her guilt trip almost worked, but then Casey came back and we both shut up.

"Uh, the proof is right there," she says, pointing to my phone. "His bed is lonely without you? What more evidence do I need? Now I'm really hurt that you didn't give me the deets."

"Bree, nothing happened." And isn't that a pile of steaming shit. Just as he promised, David was a perfect gentleman. He held me all night, his hands never straying any lower than my belly button. And when he woke up, not realizing I was already awake but terrified to move because of how wonderful his erection felt pressed against my ass, he shifted away so I wouldn't be uncomfortable by that. "Trust me, *if* anything happens, you'll be the first to know."

That seems to appease her and she goes back to the canvas she's working on stretching. Like me, Bree is a college student but she's going to the tech school and taking random courses until she finds herself. What that means is she's spending her parents' money on as many art courses as possible while she tries to convince them that majoring in art isn't a lost cause.

Me: Is that an invitation?

While I wait for David to respond, I rifle through my bag of clean clothes, trying to find something appropriate for tonight. I have no clue what we'll wind up doing, but I can guarantee that David's going to start to wonder if I show up in a t-shirt and jeans again. When I left most of my stuff behind at the school, I kept what seemed practical for summer, not what I liked. At the bottom of the bag, I find a pair of crumpled cargo shorts, but no shirt to go with them.

I tell Bree I'll be back and head out the door, hoping I'll find something at Ragtime, the local thrift store. They specialize in retro clothing, but sometimes it's possible to find something simple and timeless without spending more than a few dollars. When nothing jumps out at me, I opt for a plain white button-down shirt. I also grab a pair of sandals. For whatever reason, I've convinced myself that David will somehow learn my truth if he sees me wearing my Skechers too many days in a row. While I've never met a man who's a shoe hoarder, most have more than one pair.

When I step into the apartment, I see Bree sitting on the couch with my phone in her hand. "You're lucky

I don't want to screw things up between you and the sexpot. I so could have fucked with him on your behalf."

I snatch the phone out of her hands and flop down, not thinking twice when Bree nestles into my side to see what David has to say.

David: You seem intelligent enough that I shouldn't have to dignify that with an answer. I will pick you up at six, same place as before.

"So, should I plan on you being gone all weekend this time?" Bree asks. I lean back to look at her, nervous that somehow Casey will realize how close the two of us have gotten and think I'm trying to steal her from him as well. I ease myself off the couch so I can start getting ready. "It's fine if you say yes. We'll stash your stuff here so it's safe. I just want to know if I need to worry if you don't come back."

"I can't say for sure. I mean, David's different from guys our age," I tell her as I carefully set out all of my toiletries on the counter. Times like this, it's easy to forget that this place is nothing more than somewhere to take a shower and get out of the heat for a while. "Last weekend, I sorta freaked when he suggested going to sleep, but he didn't even try to do anything more than kiss me a couple times."

"Did you try to initiate anything with him?" Once I'm hidden behind the dark green shower curtain, I hear the lid of the toilet seat drop and know I'm not going to be able to clean myself in peace. Apparently, the fact that she and I both like guys means I'm one of the girls in her mind and we're going to chat it up. That seriously puts a crimp in my plans to rub one out while I think about how much more I wanted David to do to me.

"No. I wouldn't even know where to start with that

shit. Look, you have to realize that I'm not most guys. While my buddies were all out trying to see who could screw the most women, I was hiding out at home, praying I didn't have to fake it." Twice in less than a week, I've shared this information; both times with someone I've known less than a month. Is it odd that these people now know more about me than anyone back home or any of my classmates from last year?

"You mean you've been with girls?" Bree sounds even more dumbfounded than David had when I told him that I tried to be a good little straight boy through high school. "How does that even work?"

"Tab A goes into Slot B, just like usual," I respond sarcastically. "Seriously, I would have thought you'd understand that. Did your parents not have the birds and bees talk with you?"

"That's not what I meant and you know it. I mean, you could...you know..." As I rinse the shampoo out of my hair, I debate whether or not I should make her finish her thought. I can practically see her squirming on the other side of the curtain. "That wasn't a problem?"

I poke my head around the edge of the curtain, water dripping onto the cracked linoleum floor. "I'm sure I have no clue what you're talking about," I deadpan. "Would you care to elaborate or are you ready to hand me a towel and get the hell out of here?"

She shoves a towel at my chest and huffs out of the room. I leave her question unanswered until I'm ready to go and we're walking down to the Union. She keeps looking at me like she wants to ask again, but doesn't dare in case I make her actually say it. Seeing David waiting in the parking lot, I lean close to Bree so only she can hear me. "As long as I blocked out who I was with, I could picture a guy and get through it. But that was never as satisfying as finally being able to kiss a guy and feel his arms around me."

Bree's cheeks flush, but she recovers quickly. "Awww, that's so sappy. Damn, is it possible for that man to look any better? He's totally too clean-cut for my tastes, but he's definitely easy to look at."

We walk arm in arm across the street and I grunt in agreement. If I open my mouth to say anything, it will definitely be more sappy bullshit I'm not used to spewing. David steps away from the car with open arms and it's my turn to heat with embarrassment. I smile broadly as I go to him, but he steps to the side, wrapping his arms around Bree.

"It's good to see you again. I assume you've been keeping an eye on our boy this week, making sure he doesn't get himself into trouble?" He winks at me and I swear my heart melts into a puddle at my feet. *Our boy.* Perhaps I should be offended by being called a boy at all, but when paired with such adoration, I can't help but wonder if this is what it feels like at the beginning of a real relationship. I won't even dare think of putting a name to the emotion, other than to acknowledge that it's highly addictive.

Bree giggles and she cranes her neck to look up to David. "It's a fulltime job, but someone has to do it," she quips. She kisses my cheek and all but skips away.

David turns his attention to me and the world around me ceases to exist. I feel self-conscious in my outfit, standing next to him looking perfectly polished. Our outfits are similar, but I'm the wrinkly kid and he's the man who has his life together. As if he can see the doubt creeping into my mind, David crooks his finger under my chin, forcing me to meet his gaze.

"You look great," he assures me, leaning down to

deliver a nearly chaste kiss to my lips. "I thought we'd go for a drive and just relax tonight. What do you think?"

"Sounds good to me." I'd do just about anything, as long as it means spending time next to David.

"Is your roommate expecting you home tonight?" he asks as he pulls into traffic.

"My—" I stop myself when I realize that he thinks Bree and I live together. Close enough to the truth, I suppose, so I let it slide. "No. Actually, I think she'll be upset with me if I show up before Monday morning."

I slump in my seat, wondering if it'd be possible to disappear into the floorboards. He hasn't even asked me to spend tonight with him, even if he alluded to it, and now I'm inviting myself for the weekend.

David's phone rings and I look out the window, trying to keep myself from eavesdropping. When I glance over at him, his grip tightens on the steering wheel and I start preparing myself for a hasty departure. He's talking about something for tonight, but doesn't seem excited about whatever the person on the other end of the line is proposing.

He hangs up and I cut him off, hoping to save a bit of my dignity and avoid him actually having to blow me off. "If you need to reschedule, I understand." The little voice in my head, the one that's still about ten years old is screaming and pouting, saying it's not fair that I'm going to be cast aside, but David has a life that I can't expect to be included in. I don't think either of us are foolish enough to believe there's anything long term for us, but I was looking forward to getting some of those awkward firsts out of the way with him. After all, aren't summer flings sort of a big deal?

"What do you mean, reschedule?" David's fingers tighten around my hand. Rather than answer, I look down at the phone in the cup holder as if that's all the response that's necessary. "Oh, that. No, I'm not going to cancel my plans with you. That's not how I operate, and to do so after I've already picked you up would be inexcusable. However, Chad is once again insisting that I join them for dinner. He doesn't believe me when I tell him that I'm a grown man and don't need him coddling me."

"You two are pretty close, huh?" I ask, not knowing what else to say.

"Like brothers. I think that's part of why he hovers the way he does. Now that I've moved up here, he wants to make sure I don't get restless and move away." I wonder what it would be like to be so close to anyone. And then I'm saddened by the realization that I don't have a single person in my life like that. "What he forgets is that I fell in love with this area the first time he brought me home to meet his family. It was the end of our year of service before heading off to college and immediately, I felt like I was home. It didn't matter to me that I loved being close to my mom, this just feels right. Does that make sense?"

"I suppose." What I want to say is that I totally get it because I feel the same way, but I'm afraid to share that because now Casey's words from earlier are poisoning my mind and I'm waiting for something to happen that will make this the last place I want to be.

"Would you mind going over there? He also said he's been trying to get in touch with you, but the number he has is disconnected."

"I suppose that'd be fine." I'm sulking now, but I can't help it. I don't want another pseudo-family dinner, I want time with just David and me so I can finally figure out what, if anything, is going on between us. That will be impossible if he's off talking to Chad, leaving me in the house with Becky again. "I must have given him the wrong phone number."

"Possibly. Of course, knowing Chad as I do, he likely wrote it in that chicken scratch he calls handwriting and the numbers were illegible." David navigates through the city as if he's always lived here, taking a series of residential streets rather than the main thoroughfares. "I promise, we won't stay as late tonight and I won't let him ply me with alcohol this time."

I smile, grateful for David's sincerity. I'm fairly certain he has no clue how much it means to me when he makes such simple promises. Back home, I was laid back and my parents gave me a wide berth to do as I pleased, a fact all of my friends knew. Because of that, I was the doormat, the one they all called when they needed someone to save their asses from doing something stupid, and the one who was never asked what he wanted to do. Everyone assumed I'd be okay with whatever was going down. David doesn't know the former me, maybe that's why he's so worried about making sure I'm comfortable.

My stomach does a flip, thinking about everything we might do once we get through dinner tonight. Now that David has given me a glimpse of what it's like to touch someone, to kiss someone, I'm interested in, he's like the new toy under the Christmas tree. I want to play with him, explore him, see what he can do. But that will have to wait because the scowl on Chad's face when we pull into the driveway is a clear indication that he doesn't approve of whatever is going on between his buddy and me.

Chapter Eight

David

True to my word, I make an excuse for us to leave about an hour after the dinner table has been cleared. I have known Chad long enough to read his body language, and I am uncertain how much longer we can sit here before he opens his mouth to say something that I will regret.

"What are you doing, David?" Chad asks as he follows me out to the car. Austin is still in the house filling out some paperwork so he can officially start his new job on Monday morning.

"I am doing exactly what you have been harping on me to do for years," I respond drily. "Since about a week after you met Becky, you have been head-over-heels in love with her and it wasn't long after that that you started harping on me to find someone to share my life with. I'm not saying Austin is or is not that person, but for the first time in far too long, I'm opening my mind to the idea."

Chad picks up a basketball from beside the drive-way and starts dribbling. It wasn't long after we met when I realized he does this to have something to focus on when he's concerned the conversation is going to get deeper than he's comfortable with. "But he's so young," Chad argues. "Couldn't you find someone closer to your own age? It was bad enough the other night when I thought he was in his mid-twenties, but shit, D, he's barely legal."

I wince at the comment. Yes, it's impossible to deny the age difference, but it's something I don't think about. Austin doesn't seem like the kids I've come across through the years. I believe he has what my mother calls an old soul. "Why does his age bother you so much?" I challenge. "I know you've always done everything you could to look out for me, but I never thought you to be the type of man who would focus on something so superficial."

"Superficial?" Chad loses control of the ball and chases it into the street. "Superficial is hair color, eye color, height, that type of shit. The fact that he's fif-teen years younger than you is massive. Do you real-ize that he was probably still in diapers when we met? Or that you were already a pizza-faced kid with braces when he was born? *That*, my friend, is a major deal to most people."

Before I'm able to respond, the front door opens and Austin appears. His steps falter as he jogs down the front stairs, as if he can sense the tension radi-ating between Chad and me. Not wanting him to feel anything other than excitement and anticipation of what's to come, I reach out for Austin, carefully tuck-ing him into my side.

I narrow my eyes on Chad when his mouth tightens, holding back whatever it is he wants to say. He stiffly reaches out to shake Austin's hand, telling him to meet Bill at my place Monday morning to discuss the schedule. I mouth a quick thank you to Chad and he nods.

"Austin, why don't you get settled in and I'll be right there," I say, needing another moment alone with Chad. I wait until the door of the car is closed to plead my case with my friend. "Chad, I appreciate what you're trying to do for me, but I need you to take a step back. You should know me well enough to trust that I'm not the type of man who will go into anything without thinking it through. Austin's a good kid who needs a friend right now. I get the impression he's never had that. Not in the way it counts, at least."

"That's fine, but you can't expect me to believe that's what *you* want." Chad's right. If friendship is the only thing that can happen between us, I would accept it, but it isn't what I would prefer. Austin means something to me. In the short time since we've met, I've spent more time thinking about him than I have ever found myself doing about anyone.

"For now, we are friends. Nothing more."

Chad lifts an eyebrow. "Really? Then maybe I should be upset because you've never snuggled up to me the way you just were with the kid."

We both laugh, and I breathe a sigh of relief that the tension is beginning to lift. No matter how much I claim to live my life by my own rules, that doesn't mean I'm comfortable with the notion of Chad, or anyone else close to me, being upset by my choices.

I quickly get in the car, not wanting to give Austin any more time than we already have to start doubting whatever this might be budding between us. I can tell he's dying to know what we were talking about, but I would prefer to leave him in the dark.

"Do you want to go out for a while or would you prefer to head back to my place to watch a movie?" Needing to feel a connection to him, I reach for Austin's hand and place it on my lap.

"Not sure there's much we could do, unless you know where I could get my hands on a fake ID." The reminder of just how young he is feels like a sucker punch in my gut. It still doesn't matter, but I wonder if the difference is worrisome to Austin. There's so much he has yet to experience in life, things that I've done and have no wish to experience again.

"Let's see if we can find a movie, then," I suggest casually.

No more words are spoken on the way to my hotel. There's nothing that needs to be said in this moment because there's something so familiar about Austin that the silence is comfortable. My thumb runs lazy circles over the back of his hand, lulling him to sleep by the time I pull into the parking lot.

"Austin," I whisper, leaning over the console. He's so close, so innocent. I want to close the last few inches to nuzzle into his neck. "Come on, sleepyhead. We're here."

His eyes slowly open and Austin seems disoriented. His head lolls to the side and he flashes a coy smile. "Sorry, guess I was tired."

"I guess you were," I agree. This is uncharted territory for me and I'm feeling self-conscious. The men before Austin were flings that both of us knew wouldn't lead anywhere because we were focused on our careers. I want more than that with Austin, despite the fact that my mind is telling me all the reasons it will never work. "Let's get you inside and a bit more comfortable."

Austin's body seems to seize at my words. I wrap my hand around the nape of his neck, forcing Austin to look at me. "Relax," I urge. "Comfortable isn't some sort of code. If you need to get some rest, that's fine by me, but I don't think you want to do it in the car."

"Wouldn't be the worst place I've slept," Austin mumbles. He turns to look out the window after a brief glance in my direction. As much as I would like to find out what he means, I get the impression that would cause him to close down on me.

"Regardless, tonight you don't have to sleep in the car. Come on, let's get inside."

I quickly round the car to open Austin's door. He steps out, staring up into my eyes with a curious sense of wonder. I lace my fingers through his and once again lead him through the hotel lobby.

"Do you have any plans for the weekend?" I ask as we settle into the room. Austin slides his feet out of his sandals, placing them next to the door. I watch his movements as he walks through the room. His hand glides over the faux-granite counter before he leans against the back of one of the stools at the breakfast bar.

"No, why?" he asks, one finger tracing the pattern on the upholstery. His nerves are getting the best of him, even if he wants to relax. I make three long strides across the kitchen so I'm standing close enough to feel the heat of his body next to mine.

"Because I'd like for you to stay with me," I admit. "Starting next week, you're going to be busy with work and I'll be dividing my time between the house and getting ready to go back to work myself. That's not going to leave much time for anything else."

"Uh, okay." Austin takes one small step away from me.

"Why do you do that?" I ask, motioning for him to get comfortable on the couch. Just like last weekend, he takes a seat at the far end, curled into himself. Very aware of what I'm doing, I settle into the opposite end, this time stretching my leg along the backside of the cushion.

I'm giving him the space he needs while trying to show him what I want. Not sex. Yes, the idea of having his naked body pressed against mine is intriguing, but he's not ready for that. The way he acts, I'm not sure when he will be. What I want is for him to be at ease around me, to realize that it's okay to admit that he wants this as much as I do. I want Austin to be confident enough to let down his guard for just a little while.

"Do what?" he asks, picking at the corner of his fingernail.

"When you don't think about what you should or shouldn't want, there's this light in your eyes. It's a beautiful sight. But then, as soon as I bring up anything that *could* be seen as flirting with you, it's as if you're struggling to keep from running away from me. Why is that?"

Austin shrugs. That simple action is one that has always bothered me. He knows why, but he doesn't want to open up to me. That's too bad because I have no inclination to back off. Taking small, slow steps forward is doable, going backward is not.

"This is still weird for me," he admits. Austin wraps his arms tighter around his knees and he looks so young. I chastise myself for constantly thinking about that number when it's never factored into what I choose to do in the past. "You're the first guy I've actually done anything with and it freaks me out a bit. And there are things I can't tell you that would push you away if you knew."

The few feet separating us is too much. Rather than pull Austin into my arms, as I would like to do, I sit up, sliding to the middle cushion on the couch. I rest one hand on his knee as I reach to run my thumb across his jaw. The move catches his attention and he looks up at me.

"It's okay to be cautious, but you can't allow fear to rule your life. And I'm not sure there's anything you can say that is so awful we couldn't work through it." The corner of Austin's mouth turns up slightly. "I know this is new to you, which is why I will never make you do anything you're not ready for. But I have to admit, when I look at you, in those times when your guard is down, I know you're ready for more than you want to admit. Am I right?"

My heart races as I wait for Austin to process what I've told him and respond. "Probably." His admission is so quiet I can barely hear the single word.

Before he can second-guess himself, I lean in to kiss him. His jaw quickly relaxes as I feather kisses from one corner of his mouth to the other, silently begging him to open to me. I moan when his mouth parts and I feel his tongue drag across the seam of my lips.

Austin lowers his legs as he moves closer to me, his hands working their way from my shoulders to my neck. The kiss quickly moves from awkward and tentative to confident and needy. Austin pushes me back on the couch with a force that would be an incredible turn-on from any other man. With Austin as the aggressor, I can't help but wonder it seems manic, as if he's compelled to surrender to his libido for fear he'll realize what he's doing and stop.

For that reason alone, I push Austin away. Not forever, but for this single moment.

"I'm sorry. I thought—"

The agony in his features breaks my heart. The only thing I'm certain of right now is that I have no clue how to act around Austin to keep this from happening again. "Don't be sorry. You thought right, but now it's my turn to ask why. Why did you flip like a switch on me right there?"

"Because I don't want to be afraid anymore. And I want you to know what it means to me that you seem to be okay with the fact that I have no fucking clue what I'm doing." Austin shifts in his seat. I hazard a glance just below his waistband and see that he is definitely as turned on as I am right now. "Even if you flip out when you learn the truth, I'll always owe you for helping me take this first step."

Now I'm the one left with too much to consider. We haven't even done anything yet, and I feel as if Austin has just given me a very articulate blow-off speech. And I'm fairly certain I'm not thinking clearly because I know, logically, that I should be concerned with this obsession he has about the secrets he's holding back, but I can't bring myself to question him. I remember what it was like to be such a young man, thinking that the skeletons in my closet were going to hold me captive for a lifetime. Now, with more of that life behind me, I can laugh about what a fool I had been. And I'm not about to dwell on such things when I have a beautiful, tortured man sitting next to me.

"Austin, you need to stop thinking about the end before you even reach the start line. I hope the day will eventually come when you trust me enough to share whatever it is you're not saying. Until then, I think it would be best if we enjoy the time we have together." I hold my arms open in invitation.

Austin

David's trying so hard to make me comfortable that it's impossible for me to relax around him. I want to believe that he'll be around long enough for me to learn to trust him, but I doubt that will ever happen. After all, everyone I've ever trusted has shit on me and thrown me to the curb, why should he be any different.

Rather than listen to the bullshit in my head, I lean back to rest in David's arms. Even if this falls apart before the end of the weekend and I never see him again, I'm going to appreciate it for what it is. And then, maybe I'll be a step closer to able to consider dating.

Don't get me wrong, I'm getting addicted to the feeling of David's arms wrapped around me, the way he makes me feel grounded in a world that's otherwise adrift. The problem is we can never be anything more than what we are now; two men filling a void for one another. And hell, even that's not totally true because every time my hand creeps higher on David's thigh, hoping for more than some friendly petting or the kisses of the other night, David shuts me down. After the fourth time he lifts my hand from his leg and places it back on my own stomach, I give up trying.

The credits roll on our third television show of the night and I'm about ready to lose my shit. Twice now, he's brought me back to his hotel and I haven't gotten past first base. For better or worse, I need to put an end to the madness.

"What do you want from me?" I ask, flipping over so we're lying chest to chest on the couch. It's one of the most uncomfortable positions I've put myself in, but something tells me that I need to see the look in his eyes as he answers this question.

David pushes the hair away from my eyes, allowing his hand to rest at the back of my neck. "I want to get to know you. *Everything* about you," he admits. The raw honesty I see in his pale eyes makes it difficult to not look away. "If my interest were nothing more than physical, I could have had that with you the last time you were here, but that's not the type of man I am."

He's the one to break eye contact and my body relaxes. I fight to rebalance myself while he's lost in thought. Maybe it's the age difference, but this is one thing I've quickly learned about David; he's very cautious with his words. It's one of the reasons I don't question what he says more often than I do.

"That's not entirely true," David corrects himself. "I have often sought out the company of men for nothing more than carnal pleasure, but that is not what I want from you. I can't explain what it is, but there is something about you that I want to know. And I am willing to ignore my own desires until you are at a point where that is possible."

Maybe I should be grateful for his chivalry, but I'm not. I'm a twenty-year old virgin, at least in the ways that matter, and I'd like to fix that problem. Yes, I've had sex with a girl, but I don't really count that because it was more of an experiment. I would have been just as content slicing and dicing a dead frog in biology class for all the thrill that night gave me. It's just my luck that the first guy I have the balls to flirt with seems hung up on the safety of my virtue.

In a move so bold I'm not sure I'll ever understand what fuels me, I drag myself up David's body, my fingers digging into his hips as I grind my cock against his. The tendons in David's neck tense and I lean in, kissing and biting my way from his shoulder to his jaw. "Believe me, what you want is *definitely* possible," I whisper in his ear, bucking my hips for emphasis.

I could almost fucking cry when David curls his hands around the side of my waist. *Finally.* And then, I almost do break down like a fucking baby when he pushes me away from him.

"Austin," he sighs. I bolt back to the safety of my end of the couch. Now, I'm getting pissed off, starting to feel led on because David doesn't seem interested, despite the fact that he's invited me here for the entire fucking weekend. I bolt from the couch to the door, needing to get out of the hotel room. Needing to get away from the memories of my desperation. Away from David before I'm no longer able to keep the tears from falling.

Strong arms wrap around my waist as I slide my feet into my shoes. David pulls me back against his chest, one hand traveling the length of my chest, locking me in place against his body. "You can't run forever," David warns. "Please, come back to the couch and talk to me. One of the first skills you need to learn if you're ever going to have a successful relationship is how to communicate with the other person."

The authoritative tone in his voice tips me further off-balance. The fucker is acting like he's my damn teacher or something. Like I'm some pet project to him. *Let's teach the queer homeless kid how to act like a civilized human being.*

"Thanks for the tip," I say sarcastically. "You communicated plenty back there and this is me taking the hint."

The more I struggle to free myself from David's grip, the more his arms tighten around my waist. Not giving up. Very carefully, David turns my body so we're standing chest to chest. I lean back so I can look into his eyes. Why? I have no fucking clue.

"Austin, please come back to the couch," he practically begs. Something in the way he says please crumbles the wall I'm trying to build to protect myself. I nod weakly and the almost whimper when David lets me go.

I'm not sure what's happening to me, but I'm too tired to think about it. Not physically tired, but emotionally drained after exerting every ounce of energy I have figuring out how I can make the best of a shitty situation and flip my father the bird as I walk across the stage to claim the college degree he's sure I won't earn without his financial backing.

Chapter Nine

Austin

I've come to terms with the fact that my family has written me off. I foolishly expected to hear from my mom after I sent her a letter as soon as I got my new cell phone. I lied to myself when I said it was so she could reach me if there was an emergency back home, just like I lied to her when I told her I was staying with friends this summer. Still, it stings to know she can't be bothered to make sure her only son is okay.

Most days, I'm able to push these thoughts out of my head, but as the rest of the guys working on David's house talk about their plans for the Fourth of July weekend, I can't help but realize that I'm alone. I won't have to listen to my father rant about the state of the economy or my mother sighing heavily because it's easier than actively engaging him in a conversation. They won't grill me about the upcoming school year while I feign sleep. I always hated those trips, but this year I'd give anything to be there. Well, almost anything because I refuse to make the one statement that will thaw the frigid divide between us.

"Is something wrong?" My body tingles at the sound of David's rich voice behind me. I have to remind myself that we're not in private because I desperately want to fall into his chest and let him tell me that everything will be okay. Over the course of the past almost two months, I've opened up to him about most of my life. Unfortunately, with everything I share with him, the guiltier I feel about the one huge detail I'm keeping from him.

Thanks to Bree, I haven't had to admit how helpless I am. When he's suggested that we go to my place rather than his hotel, I've reminded him that I have roommates. When he's wanted to walk with me to get something from the apartment, I've suggested that he drive around the block a few times so he doesn't have to pay for parking. There've been a couple of close calls and I'm not sure how much longer I can keep this up, but I can't bring myself to come clean because no one who has his life together is going to stay with such a hot mess. Or worse, he'll decide that he needs to be my savior and I really don't need that shit.

"Nah, nothing that matters." Even as I say the words, I don't believe them. It *does* matter to me but I can't change it, so I'm trying to not worry about it.

"Come on, I talked to Bill and you're done for the rest of the week." David's more animated than I think I've ever seen him. It's hard to hold onto my bad mood when he's practically bouncing on the balls of his feet.

I quickly finish cleaning up the project I'm working on while David walks through the house to check on progress. He's been even busier than he anticipated and hasn't been able to be as hands-on as he originally thought he would be. There's still a fair bit of work to do, but even my untrained eye is able to see the beauty that the house will be when it's completed.

"Ready when you are," I tell him as I put away the last of my tools.

"Great! Why don't you get comfortable in the car and I will be there in a minute."

The suitcase in the backseat is the only clue I have that David has plans for our holiday weekend. I try asking him for at least a hint, but his lips are sealed. As he pulls into the parking ramp two blocks up from Bree's apartment, where he thinks I'm living, I begin to feel light-headed as the world closes in around me. I barely feel the car lurch to a stop before David's hands are on my face.

"Austin, talk to me." I can hear the worry in his voice, which is odd. Everything is fuzzy and it's hard to breathe. "Austin, look at me." This time, the firm tone in his voice is a shaky demand.

My cheeks flush as my eyes come back into focus. Panic attacks are nothing new to me, but this is the first time my body has completely shut down. The only reason I can think of is that I finally realize my time is running out. Maybe that's for the best because I'm already too dependent on David. When we're together, it's easy to forget about what my life is really like.

"Fuck, sorry 'bout that." I try to look away from him, but David's grip under my chin tightens.

"You don't need to apologize, but I do need to know what's going on. Are you not feeling well?" David's hand snakes around behind my neck, his thumb grazing the skin beneath my ear. "Austin, I believe I've been a patient man, trying to keep from upsetting you by asking too many questions, but I can't rid myself of the feeling that you are hiding something from me.

I care deeply about you, but if we are to continue exploring this relationship, I need you to be honest with me."

I take deep breaths, focusing on not blacking out again. This moment has weighed on my mind for a while now, but I somehow convinced myself it wouldn't be so soon.

"I'm afraid," I admit, my voice weak. I begin chewing on the inside of my cheek while I work up the courage to say the words I still don't speak aloud. If I don't say it, the fact that I'm homeless seems less real. But I can't not give David what he's asking for after he's been so patient with me.

"There is nothing to fear, Austin. Whatever is weighing so heavily on your mind that it causes this type of reaction, I would wager it's worse in your mind than it truly is." He leans forward so our foreheads are pressed together. I can feel his warm breath on my face and I absorb that small comfort. "Tell me and then we can work through it together."

"I've been lying to you the whole time we've been seeing each other," I admit. My voice is so low I can barely hear myself speak and I wonder if he heard me. The hiss of his breath tells me he did. Before he can kick me out of the car and send me back to the steaming shit pile that is my life, I continue. "I don't live with Bree. I mean, I do, but not how you think. Fuck, this is hard..."

I broke one of the promises I made to myself after spring break and it's going to bite me in the ass. I let myself have hope that life with David could work out when it's nearly impossible.

David's grip on my neck tightens, but not painfully so. "Austin, talk to me. Make me understand what you are beating yourself up over. Let me help you."

This isn't the first time I feel as though David sees through every veil I have in place, down to the parts of myself I think I have carefully hidden from the world. From him. Maybe even from myself. "What makes you think I need help?" I ask, crossing my arms tightly over my chest.

"Perhaps it is because I'm a highly educated man who has spent tens of thousands of dollars on a fancy degree to hang on my wall. Many of the courses related to psychology, which gives me just enough knowledge of the subject to be dangerous." He doesn't pull away from me, doesn't break contact between our bodies.

"Or maybe it's because I *see* you. I see the pieces of you that you would prefer stay in the darkness. I feel the way your body tenses when I get too close to asking questions about your present rather than your past. I hear the excuses you feed me whenever I suggest you allow me into your personal domain." I shrink back in my seat the longer he talks, wishing I hadn't asked because he does get me.

"I get the impression you see yourself as beneath me in some way. If you can give me this one thing, I will try to give you everything you need to see that I'm more like you than you can imagine," he promises. His statement fortifies me, although I'm still uncertain he can possibly understand what I'm going through.

"Okay." I sit straighter, turning to face him, squaring my shoulders to show confidence I absolutely do not feel. "I told you about my parents turning their backs on me when I came out and the way they unceremoniously dropped me off at the bus stop to be rid of me quicker. What I haven't told you…"

My voice falters. I begin to feel nauseated. Am I really doing this?

"Take your time," David urges, leaning forward to

deliver a gentle kiss to the corner of my mouth. "The only thing I ask of you right now is honesty."

"I know, but that doesn't make it any easier to say." I let out a pathetic chuckle in an effort to hide the fact that I'm terrified of his reaction. After all, I know how I would have reacted to such a revelation just a few months ago. I take a deep breath so I can say what I need to without stopping. "When school ended, my parents didn't come for me. They don't give a shit that their only son is now living on the streets, relying on the kindness of someone else for such simple things as a shower or a safe place to keep his belongings while he works to pay for the next semester of school.

"David, I don't share an apartment with Bree," I finally admit, jerking away from him so I don't have to feel his reaction. I stare at the floorboards of his car instead. "She has a place even though she sleeps at the park with the rest of us. During the day, when Casey's not around, she takes me there so I can get cleaned up and she lets me stash my stuff there while I go to work or spend time with you."

"Oh, Austin," David sighs. It's the tone my parents used to take with me when I'd disappointed them, one I'm well accustomed to at this point in my life.

"I know I should have told you sooner, but I couldn't. I'm a selfish coward and I couldn't bear to see the look you have on your face right now. I know I've fucked up everything, just like I usually do--"

"Stop!" David demands. The way the single word booms in the confines of his small car causes me to jump. "Am I disappointed? Yes. I would be lying if I said otherwise, but it's not for the reasons you're thinking. I wish you had told me sooner so I could help you. If I had known, do you think I would have dropped you off so you could stay wherever while I'm comfortable in my hotel room?"

I reach for the door handle, figuring it'll be easier on both of us if I just go. I destroyed what could have been an amazing relationship, all because I was too weak to be truthful. David's fingers dig into my biceps, keeping me from making a hasty escape.

"I don't want your pity." This is what I wanted to avoid more than him turning his back on me. In my immature mind, I truly thought I could build a relationship with him and turn my life around so it would be a moot point because then I'd know that his feelings for me weren't driven by a need to save me. I'm not going to be his charity case or the kid he can't turn his back on.

"That's good, because I don't plan to give it to you," he deadpans. "More than you know, you and I are alike. While our situations are different, I know the strength it takes to stay afloat from day to day when the current of life is against you. A weak man would have pushed for someone to rescue him. But you didn't. Honestly, I don't know that I would have had the strength to hold out as long as you have had I been in your position. The difference between us is that I had someone to guide me to a better path."

This weekend is nothing like I had planned. Austin acts as though he's waiting for me to change my mind now that I know the truth. Chad keeps eyeing me over the top of his bottle of beer as the two of us sit around the smoldering remains of a bonfire earlier in the night. He's reluctantly accepting that Austin is who I want to be with, which is the reason,

I can't talk to him about the struggle going on in my head. I don't want to give him any reason to judge Austin on a personal or professional level.

Tomorrow morning, we'll be packing up the cars to head home and I have yet to find five minutes to get Austin alone so we can talk about what happens once we're back in the real world. I have far too much life behind me to think we will be able to keep living like a happy couple, and yet I'm unwilling to drop Austin off downtown to sleep outside. Once we got past the initial discussion over his current housing arrangement, which he seems to prefer over anything directly mentioning the fact that he is homeless, Austin has slowly opened up a bit more about what he has experienced since the end of the spring semester.

Other than the insecurity that people will view him differently if they know about his plight, Austin seems to be relatively optimistic about how he plans to change his circumstances. To him, this is a bump in the road that will eventually allow him to view the world in a way other than how it was painted when he was a child. He firmly believes it will allow him to show empathy to those who are different from him. In short, he's the type of young adult the world needs more of, and I'm lucky enough to be a part of this transformation.

"Penny for your thoughts?" Chad kicks back in his chair shooting me a knowing smirk. Of course, he probably thinks I'm a lovesick fool, which may be partly the case if I'm being honest, but it's everything less intimate that warms me to the core when I think about Austin.

"You should know by now that my thoughts don't come that cheap," I chide, walking to the outdoor bar for another bottle of microbrew. "It's been good to get away this weekend. Thank you for inviting us and not busting my chops about asking Austin to join."

"He's a good kid. Bill's always talking about what a hard worker he is and he's eager to learn more. It's a shame he'll be heading back to school next month."

"I understand what you are saying, but you may want to ask him about his plans because I would bet he is hoping you will allow him to work part-time." I won't betray Austin's trust by divulging details of his life without permission, but I can't imagine he will be able to quit working and construction will pay better than most jobs. And if Chad's happy with his performance, I see no reason he wouldn't allow for some flexibility in Austin's schedule.

"David, no twenty-year-old kid is going to sit in class all morning and then bust his ass the rest of the day on a jobsite. He might try, but I don't think it'll work. He'll be too tired by the time he gets done to focus on his assignments and that should be his priority."

The sound of a door closing punctuates Chad's opinion. I sit up and see Austin hurrying through the dimly lit house. Without any explanation to my friend, I jog up the stairs and across the upper patio. I need to get to Austin because it's obvious he only heard part of the conversation.

When I step into the bedroom at the bottom of the stairs leading into the basement, Austin is busy cramming clothes into his backpack. In three long strides, I cross the room and wrap my arms around his torso, pulling him close to me. He fights to free himself, but I refuse to let him run this time. Never again will he run from me now that we've agreed to work on effectively communicating with one another.

"Just let me go," Austin demands, digging his fingers into my forearms. "I told you I didn't need you to save me, but you couldn't fucking help yourself, could you? You think I didn't know Chad wouldn't keep me on once I'm in school? I'm not the stupid kid you think I am. I knew it and I was okay with it because something was better than nothing at the time."

Rather than release Austin, I step backward with him still in my arms until we're sitting in a chair in the corner of the room. He uses the arms of the chair for leverage and almost breaks free, but not quite. "Austin, will you please listen to me? *Not once* have I called you stupid or a child, because you are neither. Although when you act like this, it makes me re-evaluate that assumption."

"Fuck you, David! I told you I didn't want your pity. You fucking promised me I meant more to you than just some charity case, but you were out there asking Chad to do something he and I both know can't happen." The door slides closed upstairs and I hear Chad padding around the kitchen. I offer up a silent prayer that the walls are sound and he's not hearing every word of Austin's outburst.

"Austin, there is a reason it is unwise to eavesdrop," I scold. "What you heard was the tail end of a conversation in which Chad was singing your praises. He doesn't want you to leave at the end of summer, but he did raise some valid points about your ability to juggle your course load on top of such a physically demanding job.

"Chad is my best friend. Had I wanted to hand you solutions to your problems on a silver platter, it would have been easy for me to betray your trust and force him to understand how badly you need the income. But I didn't, because your respect means more to me than that." Oh, but I wanted to. It's not pity that makes me wish I could do more to help Austin; it's admiration and a sense of devotion. Already, I view Austin as a piece of me and I want to protect him in every way possible. "I can't even bring myself to tell my best friend that I'm falling in love because there is so much more that I want to say but I can't because it's *your* story, not mine."

"Don't say things you don't mean," Austin whispers, relaxing enough to nuzzle his face into my neck. I'm sure we're quite the sight, stuffed into a chair that is much too small with him curled in my lap.

"I haven't so far and I don't see any reason to start now." I twist my body in the chair so I can look at Austin. His face is within inches of mine, and for the first time, I notice that his eyes are puffy and red. I wipe away the damp trails on his cheeks, kissing each one before I continue. "I have known for a while how I feel about you, but I didn't think either of us were ready to hear those words. While nothing about this weekend is what I hoped it would be, it had been my intention all along to tell you, albeit in a more romantic way."

"And then I went and fucked up your plans," Austin grumbles.

It's difficult, but I maneuver both of us so Austin is straddling my lap. He leans forward, resting his head on my shoulder and I start running my hand up and down the length of his back. "You did no such thing," I assure him. "I don't blame you for being afraid, but you faced that fear and told me the truth. You *trusted* me, and I'm relatively certain that's a gift not many receive from you. If anything, that only solidified my determination to make sure you know that you are loved. I love you, Austin, and nothing you can say is going to change that for me."

Chapter Ten

Austin

At some point, I'm going to wake up from this dream. I know this because every dream this amazing ends sometime. I couldn't say the words back to David when he told me he loves me last night; not because I don't feel the same way, but because I can't allow myself to admit that on top of everything else this weekend. I want the first time I say those words to someone to be a happy moment, not one where my emotions are so raw it's physically painful.

On the other hand, now that he's gone there, I can't imagine not being with him. I didn't fight him when he told me that I'm spending the rest of the summer with him, and I even let him walk with me to find Bree and Casey so I could get the rest of my stuff.

Bree was practically doing cartwheels when I told her the news, although I could see a slight twinge of envy creeping to the surface. She's as sick of the streets as I am, but she's so stupid in love with Casey that she won't tell him as much because of his ridiculous pride. Casey said he was happy for me, but the words felt hollow and judgmental, like I'm a bad person for letting David take care of me. And David...well, let's just say he looked around with some combination of disgust and shock at where I've lived since the end of May.

But none of that matters right now as I sit on the bed watching David rearrange his drawers so I don't have to live out of my bags.

"Tomorrow, you need to call the school to see if you can reclaim the rest of your belongings," he urges as I finish folding the last of my clothes. Luckily, this hotel has on-site laundry because I couldn't imagine putting them away smelling like the oh-so pleasant blend of scents they absorbed downtown.

"I'm sure they threw everything into a dumpster when they cleared out the rooms." Which sucks because I'm sick of looking at the few items I have here. Not to mention there are some things I wish I had had the room to bring with me. "But it was a good thought," I add, not wanting to seem ungrateful.

"Actually, I looked online while you were down in the laundry room and their policy is to hold all belongings for sixty days. You're just under that right now, so if you call tomorrow, we can ask Chad to help us move whatever you had to leave behind." While I'm still not entirely comfortable with David taking charge this way, I have to admit it's nice to have someone looking out for me. I would have assumed it was a lost cause without even trying to find information on policies. And had I known I had that much time to claim my property, I would have been too nervous to ask

David to help me store it because the truth is I still have no clue what the future holds for me.

I'm at the point that I should be able to make the 'parental contribution' payment on my own, but only if I forego living on campus. It would be nice to have three hot meals each day and a warm bed at night, but at this point their luxuries I can't afford. I'll simply have to hope David doesn't get sick of my shit and put me out on my ass or that Bree keeps her apartment and will let me hang out there when the weather gets cold.

"Only if you don't mind," I respond. "I don't want Chad to feel obligated and this room isn't all that big. I don't want to junk it up with all my shit."

David sits on the edge of the bed, patting his leg. I lay my head on his thigh, the way I've grown to love doing when we're watching television together. He cards his fingers through my hair, which I really need to find time to get cut. "Chad will help you because he considers you more of a friend than most of his other employees. And I want to walk into the room and see reminders that I'm not in immediate danger of growing into a lonely old man as my mother keeps warning me is bound to happen."

He doesn't talk much about his mom, but I wonder what it's like to have even one parent who is so loving and accepting. It'd be nice to hear more because he seems to care deeply for her, but I won't ask any questions that could lead to him asking more about my own family. He knows we don't get along now, but that doesn't mean he won't ask about my childhood.

"You're not *that* old," I tease, trying to keep the mood from getting heavy. "But seriously, you should know that I have a ton of stuff. I hate to admit it, but before all of this, I may have had an addiction to building the biggest wardrobe possible. And there are at least two totes filled with nothing but books I accumulated over the course of the year."

"Well, then I guess you will have to go through them and whatever you don't need right this minute can go to the storage unit with most of my worldly possessions."

David runs his hand down my back, gently tugging at the hem of my t-shirt. We've been playing this game since we met, trying to learn the feel of every inch of the other's body, but it's not enough anymore. David told me he loves me and I know I'm falling for him, whether I will admit that to myself or not, and tonight I'm going to do everything in my power to finally seal the deal. I know what it's like to feel a man's hand or lips wrapped around my cock, and I fucking love the way David can practically screw me into the mattress with his fingers, but if I don't get to feel his thick cock filling my ass to the point I think I'm going to explode, I might lose my shit. Patience is a virtue I don't possess, and David seems intent to make me learn to wait.

I bend my knees and hook my leg behind the neatly folded piles of clothes, sending them flying across the room. David shakes his head and chuckles as he glances at the clothes strew all over the floor. "You're an impatient boy tonight, aren't you?" he chides.

My body stiffens, uncomfortable with that particular term of endearment. I doubt he means anything by it, but to me, it's a reminder of the differences in not only our ages, but where we are in our lives.

"What's wrong?" David asks, shifting my body on the bed so he can lie next to me.

"You can call me whatever you want, but please, not that," I beg. David pushes my shirt up my chest, lifting my upper body off the bed long enough to pull the shirt over my head. Without answering my request, he leans over and starts kissing and biting my side. I let out a needy moan, my hips arching in anticipation that he'll keep moving lower. My insecurities melt away as David tells me how beautiful my body is, how he loves tasting me. Every time we've been together, he's proven to be a vocal lover, using his words to assure me of his feelings.

David makes quick work of undoing the button and zipper on my shorts before pushing them down my legs, leaving me on display for him. The way he looks at me as if my body is a gift meant just for him is enough to make my cock grow painfully hard. I know what happens next, and my erection throbs waiting to feel the heat of his mouth.

"No, don't stop," I whine when David gets up from the bed. I listen as he starts the water in the bathroom, letting the water heat while he returns to the bedroom. I lick my lips as I watch him strip and follow him into the shower.

The sound of the glass door closing after we step into the steam echoes through the small room. I watch with rapt attention as David pours body wash onto the washcloth before instructing me to turn around. "I'm going to take care of you tonight," David promises me. I moan, trying to remember a time I've felt so relaxed.

"David." The single word seems to catch on the ball of nerves gathered in my throat. My legs tense as David reaches the base of my spine as he kneels behind me. There's no time to think before his soap-slicked fingers trail between my ass cheeks. "Please...more..." I beg.

"Be patient and I promise it'll be worth it." David places his hands on my hips and turns my body so I'm facing him. It's fucking torture to have his face so close and yet so far from where I want to feel him. As if he knows how painful this is for me, David takes his time running the washcloth up one leg and then the other, through the crease of my hips, allowing his fingers to barely graze the hot flesh of my cock.

He stands, giving the same attention to my chest, torturing one nipple and then the other. Finally, he tosses the washcloth into the corner, pushing me under the spray of the showerhead. "There, that wasn't so bad, was it?" he taunts.

In response, I drop to my knees, wincing at pain radiates from my kneecaps. I run my tongue through the slit to collect the salty pre-come before sliding my lips down his shaft until I can't take anymore without gagging. His cock feels heavy against my tongue as I repeat the motion, each time trying to take him deeper. David's body shifts as he reaches for the towel bar on the sidewall of the shower. I hum, pleased with myself for nearly bringing the man to his knees and his fingers twist tightly in my hair. The pressure is nearly painful, but I use that sensation to bolster my confidence because David is obviously enjoying himself.

"Austin...stop..." David pants. He pulls me up from the floor as he reaches to turn off the water. We barely take the time to dry off in our haste to get back to the comfort of the bed.

The David in front of me isn't the tentative, concerned man I've gotten used to. His eyes are on fire with desire and I shift uncomfortably under his predatory gaze. My breathing becomes shallow and labored as he stalks across the room and pushes me to the bed.

"Is this too much?" he asks, bracing himself on his elbows so we're only touching from the waist down. I roll my hips, urging him to keep going. "I've wanted you for so long, but you have to tell me this is what you want."

"Fuck, yes!" I shout, digging my fingers into his shoulders to pull him toward me. David resists momentarily and I can see him trying to pull back, to slow down and make this something other than a hasty fuck between two horny men. What he fails to realize is that is exactly what I want right now. I don't need hearts and butterflies or roses and chocolates, I simply want David to trust me enough to claim me.

I buck my hips off the bed, grinding our erections together as I tug on his hair. "Stop trying to make this perfect for me. It already is because it's with you. I love that you try to take care of me and make sure I'll never regret anything we do, but that's not possible. It's *because* it's you that I know I'm ready for this."

He stares at me for a moment before sealing his lips over mine. I open my mouth, forcing my tongue between his lips. If he doubted my words, I'm hoping to erase that hesitation with my actions.

David breaks the kiss, climbing across the bed to his nightstand. I can't help myself when his hips are right next to my head and I roll on my side, once again sucking him into my mouth. His back arches as he begins thrusting deeper toward my throat. For the first time, I'm able to take him fully to the hilt and I make a mental note to remember this position. I swallow around David's cock and he gasps.

Far too soon for my liking, David sits back on his heels leaving my body once again wanting him. "You keep that up and I'm going to spend the rest of the night trying to recover," he warns me. "Remember, I'm not as young as you. I can't do marathon sex anymore."

Bitterness rises in my throat at the notion that he

may have had marathon sex ever. It's ridiculous since I know he's not a virgin, but I don't want the reminder that he's been with other men while every ounce of my experience has been thanks to him. Seeing my fallen expression, David leans forward, running his thumb along my jaw.

I throw my arm over my eyes, shielding him from seeing every doubt creeping back into my mind. David pulls my arm away, hovering barely an inch away from my face. "Stop overthinking. If the difference in our ages mattered, you would have known it long before now. I don't give a shit that you're younger than me, but twice now, you've pulled away when I made an off-handed remark."

"I know," I sigh. And I do know. Every time age has become a factor, it's been because of me. "I guess I still can't figure out what someone like you is doing with someone like me."

David quickly pulls what he needs out of the nightstand drawer and settles himself so he's straddling my hips. His hands knead my tense shoulders as he stares into my eyes. "Austin, I'm with you because you are funny, smart and incredibly sexy. The way I see it, if I didn't make up my mind to be with you soon, you would have realized that you can do better than me."

"That wouldn't happen," I promise him. Even if he'd made me wait a year, I probably would have because David has a way of not only making me forget about the shitty life I'm trying to leave behind, but also makes me feel like I can achieve my goals.

One finger presses against my lips, sealing them shut while David speaks. "You say that, but there is an entire world out there you have never been able to explore. I know being in a relationship scares you, but the truth is, it terrifies me as well. I don't know what

I would do if you left now that I've given in to these feelings."

Too much talking. Seriously, less than five minutes ago we were on our way to what I have no doubt would have been an epic fucking session, and now I feel like we're on an episode of those cheesy talk shows my mother loved to watch when I was younger. I wouldn't be shocked if some fancy shrink walks into the room to dissect every word we're exchanging.

"Uh, could we talk about this later?" The corner of David's mouth lifts in a quirky grin. He rocks his body back and forth, bringing both of our slightly deflated erections back to full attention. "I can think of a lot of things I'd rather be doing right now."

David spreads my legs wide, settling himself between them. One at a time, he picks up my feet to move them closer to my ass, leaving me on full display. I close my eyes as one hand cups my balls while the other starts stroking my shaft. His middle finger works my taint and I think I'm going to go insane from trying to process all of the sensations that are bound to make me explode all over his hand.

"You deserve to be loved," he says, leaning over to add the pressure of his teeth around my tight nipple to the sensation overload. "You deserve to be taken care of, all the time," he adds before moving his mouth to the other side of my chest.

"And I hope you understand that I will never take the gift you're giving me for granted." I'm so caught up in his words that I didn't notice his hand leave my body and I'm taken by surprise when one slicked finger breaches the ring of muscle in my ass. He thrusts it deep as he bites my lower lip. "Thank you for trusting me."

David

As I watch Austin's body writhe beneath mine, I begin to wonder why I insisted on waiting so long for this. Never before have I been the type of man to hold out for two months before taking the final step in a physical relationship. Now, that's not to say I have been a whore, but I never would have thought I would place so much value on the needs of my partner that I ignored every carnal desire for his benefit.

I slide a second finger inside his body, curling to brush against his prostate. The action nearly causes him to levitate above the mattress. "You're always so responsive," I praise him.

"Please, David! Shut up and fuck me before I explode!" Austin screams. Knowing this is his first time, I want to make sure I work to open him so he can enjoy the feeling of being filled, but I feel the last frayed nerve in my body snap and I need to take him. Now.

I sit back on my heels, my cock twitching as I watch him watching me roll the condom down my length. I've always loved the way his eyes shimmer, but tonight, they're hooded and nearly black with lust. "Grab your legs behind your knees," I instruct him. He does, and then pushes his legs back so he's nearly doubled over on himself. "Hold it just like that. This is going to hurt at first, but I promise to go slow."

"Less talking," he pants. "More fucking."

He glares at me defiantly, practically daring me to continue holding out on him. Now that we're here, I have no plans to stop. I need him too much, possibly more than I have ever wanted another man in my life. I stroked my cock slowly, slathering my shaft with enough lube to hopefully minimize Austin's discomfort before aligning the head of my cock to his entrance. When Austin lifts his hips, trying to rush me, I grab hold of his thighs. "Easy, baby," I whisper. "Stroke yourself and bear down when the pressure gets to be too much, okay?"

Austin's wobbly nod is all the response I get. I bite my lower lip hard enough to draw blood as I breach his body. I knew he would be tight, but this is almost too much. His breath turns to quick pants as I inch my way deeper inside his hot channel. Once I'm completely buried in him, I lean over, devouring his mouth while he gets used to the stretch of me inside his body.

"Holy fuck," Austin groans. "You feel...fuck...David, need you to move." He starts bucking his hips as much as he can while bearing my full weight. "Please...need you."

"Keep stroking yourself," I tell him as I sit up and start slowly thrusting in and out. "You feel so good. Perfection," I praise. I reach beneath his body, taking one firm cheek in each hand, lifting him to change positions slightly so the head of my cock bumps against his prostate on each stroke. I know I've hit my mark when I hear Austin's pleading turn to incoherent screams and moans.

"David, I'm gonna blow," he warns me. I kiss him as I quicken my pace, whispering encouragement against his neck for him to let go if he needs to. "Oh, God!" he screams as his entire body tenses and ropes of come coat both of our bodies.

His ass convulsing around my shaft brings me to a quicker than desired climax. My body still as I come buried deep inside his body, which is exactly where I would stay forever if it were possible.

I look up and see Austin looking utterly sated. I pull

out, chuckling when he whimpers at the sensation of being empty. I understand the feeling well. I leave the bedroom, quickly returning with a washcloth to clean both of us before ducking under the covers with him. I pull Austin's body to mine, tenderly kissing his shoulder. "Are you okay?" I ask, slightly nervous because he hasn't said a word yet.

"No," he chuckles. "I think you fucked my brains out and they fell on the floor."

"Does that mean you don't want to do that again?" I tease. Austin flips over before I have time to react and sits on my stomach.

"You'd fucking better do that again. And often." He pinches my nipples, punishing me for suggesting that this might have been the only time. "That was fucking amazing."

I wrap my arms around Austin's back, pulling him so his body is covering mine. "I'm glad you enjoyed yourself. Now, let's get some sleep because we both have to be up early tomorrow. I can drop you off in the morning, but we'll have to stop at the front desk and get you a key so you can take the bus back here. I have a meeting for work and it's possible I won't be able to get back here until about nine tomorrow night."

"It's okay. I can just hang with Bree and Casey and then you can call me when you're ready to head back." This suggestion puts me in an awkward place. On the one hand, I understand that Austin is friends with them and I don't want to isolate him from his peers any more than he already has been, but on the other, I can't be sure he won't change his mind about staying with me if he goes there.

"If that's what you really want, but I thought you would prefer to come back and relax in the air conditioning until I get back," I say, trying to sound nonchalant. I run my fingers along Austin's spine, loving how responsive he is even now. "Besides, these meetings will become more frequent as the summer goes on and I don't want you feeling as though you're only welcome when I am here. I want this to be your home, too. Well, as much of a home as either of us have right now." I chuckle, hoping I haven't completely offended him.

Austin buries his head in my chest and I think he's going to fall asleep on me. It wouldn't be the most comfortable position, but I would suffer through the discomfort to be close to him. "Okay."

The single word sounds more like a concession than an agreement. I decide to take it as a small victory for the night because we could go around in circles until it's time to leave otherwise.

Chapter Eleven

Austin

Even though David warned me his late nights were going to become more frequent, it doesn't make it any easier to sit around the hotel room and wait for him to get back. When he's here, he keeps me distracted so I can't think about the fact that I'm letting him support me. But when I'm alone, I feel on edge and out of place. If it's this bad now, when we're still in the hotel, I can only imagine what it'll be like next week after we move into the house.

Tonight, I'm trying to concentrate on the course catalog so I can jump online tomorrow morning to register. Thanks to a healthy bonus from Chad, supposedly given to everyone on the crew for managing to finish David's house ahead of schedule, I'll be able to take a full course load for at least one more semester. I'll have to commute every day, but I found out that I could get an exemption from the sophomore housing requirements by filling out independent student paperwork. That's one more pile of papers I absolutely have to fill out tonight so I can return them tomorrow.

I'm not one-hundred percent comfortable with squatting in David's house, but he won't hear of any other solution. He even offered to give me the second spare room rather than turn it into a guest room if I felt more comfortable having my own space. That led into a huge disagreement because he seemed so willing to give me my own space that my insecurities got the better of me and saw it as him distancing himself. He countered with the point that I'm the one who is resisting admitting what I'm feeling, not him, and I couldn't disagree. In the end, we wound up compromising that I will use the spare room to store some of the stuff I don't need on a regular basis and I'll have a desk in there for when I need to study, but otherwise, we'll share his bedroom.

I lean back to grab the remote control from the end table and wind up spilling papers all over the damn floor. Apparently, staples and paperclips were the office supplies overlooked thanks to budget cuts at the school. For as much as I'm shelling out between out-of-pocket costs and loans I'll be paying off until I retire, you'd think they could clip this shit together. I slide off the couch and start organizing everything back into neat stacks and then sorting them in order of importance.

When the door buzzes, signaling that David's back, I'm taking one last look at my dream schedule for the semester. I'll be taking eighteen credits, which is a bit much, but that's what I'm allotted thanks to my financial aid package so I'll find a way to do it.

"What's that?" David asks, pointing a bottle of beer toward the stack of papers as he toes off his wingtip dress shoes. David is always sexy, but there's something about seeing him padding around the room after work that makes me rock hard instantaneously. My body is already stirring, knowing that next he'll take off his tie and then unbutton the top three buttons on his silky black dress shirt, exposing the dark brown curls on his chest. "Austin?"

I look up and see David smirking at my inattention. "Sorry," I say meekly, picking up the stacks and moving them to the breakfast bar. "I have to register for classes tomorrow and I'm trying to get everything ready. If it's anything like spring, I'll be fighting to get onto the system half the morning and don't want to waste any time, otherwise I'll have to pick classes I don't really want or need."

David looks at the front of the course catalog and the color drains from his face as he scrubs the back of his neck. "You're at the university?" he asks, taking a long draw off his beer.

"Yeah, you knew that," I respond defensively. I pull out one of the stools and sit to keep working. The couch is more comfortable, but if I'm sitting that close to David, I won't want to focus on what needs to be done because doing him is much more satisfying than paperwork.

"Yes, but I assumed you would transfer to the tech college to reduce the financial burden." I bristle, wondering if he thinks I'm foolish for not wanting to transfer and then transfer back.

"I considered it, but I won't be eligible for guaranteed placement in my major if I do that. The guaranteed transfer is only for new freshman who complete the full two years at the tech college and declare their intent to transfer."

David nods as if he understands, but he still seems

unsettled. Even worse, he's not looking at me. "Can I see what you're planning to take?"

"Uh, okay." I hand him the worksheet, slightly pissed by the way his brow furrows as he reads through the list. He's been understanding so far about my need to stand on my own, but I'm wondering if this is going to be the moment when he starts trying to use his age and experience as a way to influence my decisions. Roof over my head or not, that'd be a fucking deal breaker.

"You need to find a different session for this class," he demands, pointing to my Tuesday/Thursday Sociology class.

"Um, no, I don't," I bite back, snatching the paper out of his hands. "It was a pain in the ass to build this schedule and I happen to think that will go well with my major."

I fucking knew better than to think this could work between us. He's assuming he knows what's best for me because he's been there and done that. Well *fuck that.* I storm into the bedroom to get my backpack. For the second time, I'm probably abandoning everything I own, but I survived once, I can do it again. All I need is some clothes, my phone, my laptop and the stuff for school.

David follows me into the closet and wraps his strong arms around my body, immobilizing me. "For once, would you stop and listen to me?" he growls into my ear. Fuck, if I wasn't so pissed off at him, which would be sexy as hell. But I'm not turned on, I'm furious. I need to get out of here. I dig my fingers into his forearms, trying to break free. "Austin, stop!"

My body stills, unaccustomed to this particular tone from him. "Just let me go. I knew this would happen eventually and I suppose I should be glad it's now, before I get used to having a place to call my own," I cry. Like a fucking baby, David's reduced me to tears over this shit. I haven't told him yet, but I'm completely, madly in love with him and it's breaking my heart to leave, even if I know it's what's best for me.

David lifts me off the ground and carries me into the living room. "Sit," he demands as my feet hit the floor. "As much as I love you, I'm getting sick of these childish games you play sometimes."

The criticism slices right through me. I flop onto the couch, curling up in the opposite corner from where he always sits. "You knew when you met me that I'm still a child," I retort, which I know is about the most immature thing I could say.

"Stop, petulance isn't a good look on you." David hurries to the fridge, bringing back a soda for me and another bottle of beer for himself. "I'm not saying you shouldn't take Sociology. I think it's a great course, but you can't take that particular session."

"Why does it matter which session I take?" I watch David grab the course catalog and open it to the timeline page.

"Who is the instructor of that course?" he asks, pointing to the line I have highlighted.

I look at the instructor name and my jaw drops. "You're D. Becker, aren't you?"

David nods, taking the book from my hands. "Now, do you understand why I'm 'forcing' you to choose a different session?" He makes air quotes around the word forcing, because he really isn't making me do shit.

"Is it going to matter when I take it? David, I'm not going to risk you getting in trouble for dating a student. I can't do that to you." I stand and start pacing around the room. "And why in fuck's name didn't you tell me you were a damned professor? You said you were a teacher. Teacher implies something below college. God dammit!"

I slam my bottle of soda on the breakfast bar and it erupts all over the papers. I quickly start shaking them off, finally giving up and hoping that the business center in the lobby is open all night so I can print my own copies of the paperwork.

This is a fucking nightmare.

"I never said I was a teacher," David says softly. "You asked me what I did for a living and I said I taught; which I do."

I don't turn around to look at him, but I can hear his footsteps as he crosses the room to me. He wraps his arms around my waist and holds me, tenderly this time, as he explains. "You're already freaked about the fact that you're younger than me and because you were homeless and worked on building my house. You're *obsessed* with all of the differences between us and I didn't want to add one more."

He kisses the hollow behind my ear, nips at the tendon along the side of my neck. Slowly, I feel myself relax into his embrace. "You're right, but now I feel like an idiot *and* I'm freaking out about this. You're a fucking professor! I can't date a professor."

"Why not?" he asks, leading me back to the couch. "As long as you're not in my class and I'm not the head of the department or your adviser, there won't be an issue."

"Are you sure?" I ask, doubtful that it could be so simple. David stretches out on the couch and I take my place laying against his chest.

"I'll double check tomorrow, but that's the policy at most campuses. Think about it, if faculty and students weren't allowed to date, no spouse or signifi-

cant other of a professor could enroll at the school."
As usual, David makes sense. I can't help but wonder
how many of these tantrums he'll sit through with me
before he realizes that he's too old to put up with my
shit. "And as for that class, go in tomorrow morning
and talk to someone in the admissions office. They're
usually pretty good about helping students plan out
their schedules.

"My recommendation would be to find a different
course for that slot so they can't try to place you in
my class. That's the only 100 level course I'm teaching
this year, so it's not as though you will have to dodge
any other times."

I'm ticked that I've wasted most of my evening, but
now that David's pulled me from the edge of a nervous
breakdown, I'm glad we figured this out now, rather than once the school year started. The responsible thing to do would be to get up and finish my paperwork, but I decide that can wait as David drapes
his arms over my shoulders and starts massaging my
chest. After all, who am I to question his wisdom?

David

Austin has been a changed man since the other
night. I thought he was going to run as fast as
he could when I told him to change his schedule, but he proved me wrong by sitting down to hear
me out. Now, there's an eerie sense of calm about him,
as though he has decided that he will no longer fight
for all the ways our relationship could potentially fail.
That should allow me to breathe easier at night, but in
reality, it has left me waiting for an outburst that will
make the one about school seem like little more than

a polite conversation.

"I think that's everything," Chad declares, pulling down the rolling door on the moving truck. It didn't take long to move everything from the storage unit to the house because most of my furniture was left behind in Mississippi. I couldn't justify the expense of moving second-hand furniture to move into a brand new house. While it goes totally against every frugal bone in my body, this is my castle, the home I've dreamed of owning my entire life, and I want to have belongings that no one else has previously owned for the first time in my life. I want this to feel like home when I walk through the doors.

"Thanks," I say, leaning against the side of the truck, taking a look at the front of the house with warm light glowing in every window for the first time. Austin appears in one of the two living room windows, waving for us to come inside, which means he and Becky have dinner ready. "You've helped more than you'll know," I add, nodding to where Austin is still watching the two of us.

"Oh, I think I know and don't you think I won't call in a favor or two down the line." Chad laughs. The sound quickly dies and Chad starts shifting from one foot to the other uncomfortably. He wrings the back of his neck, as if he wants to say something but doesn't know if that is a wise decision.

"Spit it out, already," I urge.

"Look, I know things are going good for you and the kid, so I'm only going to ask this once and then I'll let it drop." Becky opens the front door, hollering for us to get inside or go hungry, so we start walking over the cobblestone path to the house. "Are you sure you know what you're doing? I'm not going to insult you by saying I think you're trying to rescue the kid because

I can tell you're head over heels in love, but what happens when he turns twenty-one and wants to go to the bars and you have to sit home grading papers late into the night?"

I bristle at the way Chad keeps referring to Austin as 'the kid'. I've learned that's a touchy subject for Austin and don't want my friend accidentally offending him in our home. And yes, I consider this to be *our* home despite the fact that only my name is on the deed. "If and when that happens, *Austin* and I will work through it," I respond curtly, emphasizing Austin's name. I'll use it excessively if that's what it takes to get Chad to drop this nickname he seems prone to using.

"It's taken time for me to convince Austin that I'm not going to get tired of his youth, and I will admit that I have thought about the points you brought up." Everyone sees me as being obsessively methodical, but the reality is that I have the same insecurities as everyone else. The difference is that I won't allow that to hold me back from reaching for what I decide matters in my life. "Sometimes, I look at him and wonder why he wants to be with someone like me, when he could have his pick of any guy on campus. I can't allow him to see that because he's fragile enough for the both of us. If he wants to spend time with his peers, I will encourage that behavior as long as I'm the one he comes home to at night. Although I dare say that's highly unlikely given what I know about him."

"Just...be careful, David. You've always had a soft spot in your heart and I don't want to watch him put that through the meat grinder." Chad stops a few yards from the front door, appraising the workmanship of the house. He drapes his arm over my shoulder in what could be seen as slightly intimate to those who don't know this is how we've always been and I allow my gaze to trail his. "I don't often get to enjoy our projects once they're done. My guys did a damn good job."

"Did you think I would have entrusted them to something this important if I didn't know you only hired the best?" I ask, motioning for Chad to head inside. The front door opens again with a final warning from Becky. Chad follows his wife, but I stand on the porch for a moment, breathing a sigh of relief at knowing I've crossed one more goal of my list. Two if you include finding someone to share my life with.

Chapter Twelve

Austin

With David off to some conference for the week, the house is too quiet. When he's here, he always has music streaming through the sound system, much to my dismay when he's in the mood for classical. I can't tell him, but right about now I feel lonelier and more desperate than I was when I lived on the streets. No matter how many times he reminds me that this is my home as much as his and that he wouldn't have asked me to move in if he wasn't crazy about me, it doesn't feel like home.

It feels about like when I used to go visit my Uncle Joe in Lancaster. He was the one family member I didn't mind spending part of the summer with, but I always felt like I was invading his space. I'd take extra care when leaving a room to make sure it was the same as when I had entered it and everything seemed stiff. Just like this house when David's not around.

My cellphone rings and I have to rush up the stairs to reach it before it goes to voicemail. It's earlier than David's called the past two nights, but he's the only one who really uses this number. "Hello?" I answer, out of breath.

"Austin, is that you?" Thank God the phone was on my bed because I'm not sure my knees would hold me up right now. I damn near break down into tears at the sound of the voice on the other end of the line. "Hello?"

"Yeah, Mom. It's me." I want to be pissed off that it took her three months to call me, but I can't. I'm back to being that little boy who would give anything to hear his mother praise him. "What's wrong?" My voice cracks and I take a few deep breaths, hoping I can hold my shit together.

"Nothing, Austin." She sounds just about as raw as I feel. "I...I can't talk long, but I needed to know you're okay. Are you? Okay?"

"Yeah, Mom. I'm good." It's not really a lie, because I'm far better than I expected to be. I have a man who loves me, who will push me to be the best person I can be, and he puts up with my shit. Let me tell you, that alone makes him worthy of sainthood sometimes.

"Good." There's a long pause after that single word response. "I have so much I want to tell you, but there's not time right now. Will you be around later this week? I know you probably have a job and your own life now, but I really need to see you."

I'm torn over how to respond. The hurt part of me wants to tell her to fuck off, that she's had months to get in touch with me and didn't care. But the sheer panic in her voice won't let me turn her away. I'd be well within my rights to show her what it feels like to be shunned, but that thought doesn't offer me any peace.

"I'll be home this weekend," I offer. I won't meet her before then, because I don't know that I'm strong enough to do this without David. And if she wants to talk to me in person, she's going to have to understand the role he plays in my life. "Mom, I'm willing to see you, but you have to know that I'll be bringing my boyfriend along. He's the only person who's given a damn about whether I have food to eat or a place to stay and I won't keep this from him."

The seconds tick by as my mother sobs quietly into the phone. Hearing how this is affecting her threatens my resolve. I want to be an asshole, but she's my mom. Memories of my childhood stream through my mind; some bolster my perception of my parents as uncaring and willing to throw away their own son, but the ones from when I was younger tell me a much different tale. My mom spending time with us kids while my father was out of town. That's a woman I haven't let myself think about in a long time, because it cuts too deep to think about how such a loving woman would turn her back the way she did.

"That would be nice, Austin," she weeps. The words are barely audible and stilted by her tears. No way in hell is my mom this good at acting. "I don't deserve anything, but I hope you will understand after we sit down. I hope you'll be able to forgive me someday and I'll get to know this man you seem so smitten with."

"Mom, I have to go, but I will call you Thursday to figure out the details." I have to get off the fucking phone before I lose it. Until I know what's going on in my mother's head, I won't let her see the pain her actions have caused me. Hell, I don't know that I will ever share that with her because if she's up to something now, I won't give her the satisfaction and if she has a legitimate reason for her actions, I won't punish her that way. "I love you, Mom."

Her sniffling tears turn into what I imagine to be body-wracking sobs. "I love you more than you know, Austin. Thank you for being a better man than I could have hoped for," she praises when she's able to get control of her emotions. "I'll talk to you later this week."

I sit on the edge of the bed, staring at the phone without seeing it for a long time. I'm so numb by the time it rings again that I feel the vibration against my palm more than hear it ringing. "Hello?"

"Austin, are you okay? What's wrong?" I'm never speechless, but this is the second time tonight I'm unable to answer someone. This time, it's because I'm overcome with the realization of how much David grounds me. Just hearing his voice over the phone steadies me.

"I don't know," I respond timidly. "My mom called me tonight..."

I hate that David's not here with me. I need to feel his arms around me. "Do you want to talk about it?"

I nod, as if he can see me. I lie back on the bed, wrapping my arms around David's pillow as I tell him about the bizarre phone call. He doesn't say anything until I get to the end of my story. Even then, he's quiet and I wonder if he thinks I should have handled her differently.

"I think it will be good for the two of you to clear the air," he finally responds. "I do, however, think it would be beneficial if this first meeting is on neutral ground. Why don't we drive to Saint Paul when I get home Friday morning and she can meet us there?"

"You'd do that for me?" I don't want mom making the eight hour drive on her own, but I wasn't about to ask David to drive most of the way to her.

"There's nothing I wouldn't do for you, Austin. I thought you understood that by now." I close my eyes, picturing David lying next to me in the bed as I inhale deeply to pick up his scent. "Find a hotel where she'll be comfortable and make a reservation for us. If you look in the top left drawer of my desk, you'll find a credit card you can use to secure the room."

"David, I can't ask you to pay for this trip. I appreciate it, but I can take care of it."

"We can discuss payment when I get home, but that doesn't change the fact that you need a card to make the reservation." I'm not an idiot, I know he's not going to let me pay him for the room, but I appreciate the fact that he's at least pretending to be open to the idea. I know that sounds fucked up, but it helps me not feel like a total leech. "I have one more function to attend tonight, so I have to go. Are you going to be okay now?"

"Yeah, I'm good," I assure him. "I might go spend some time with Bree and Casey tonight, just to get out of the house. It's too quiet when you're gone."

"That sounds good. Take the car in case you're out late and call me when you get home." The way David worries when I go downtown on my own, you'd think we live in Chicago and I'm headed to the south side. But, I let him get away with it because it proves he cares. "I love you, Austin."

"Love you, too." The words are out of my mouth before I know what I'm saying and I feel like a shit. It's the first time I've admitted my feelings to him, and it's over the fucking phone. *Really fucking romantic.*

"I'm happy to hear it," David chuckles. "I'll talk to you late tonight."

David

Austin is trying to downplay his nerves, but I can practically feel the tension radiating off his body as we make our way through central Wisconsin. His mother has been cryptic in her communication, which led Austin to coming up with every worst-case scenario possible. Everything from his father pressuring his mother into meeting Austin in order to sabotage his efforts to stay in school all the way to his mother being terminally ill and she's trying to make amends before it's too late.

The true purpose of her sudden interest in his life is probably somewhere between those two extremes, but Austin refuses to listen to reason. After one hundred miles of watching Austin's leg bouncing in the passenger seat, I reach over and dig my fingers into his knee.

"Austin, relax. We'll be there in a few hours and you can return to pacing around the hotel room." My attempt at a joke falls flat. Austin intertwines our fingers and looks down at them. He does this sometimes, typically when he needs a reminder that what we share is real and I'm not going anywhere. Had my parents abandoned me, I might feel the same way. "Do you know where you would like to go for dinner?"

"I don't care. There are some good places near the hotel, but I doubt I'll be able to eat much." Food is one topic Austin's usually enthusiastic about, so I know he's got to be in a bad headspace.

"How about steak? I will have to check, but I think we'll be close to a great steakhouse." I refuse to let Austin pull into himself. If I have to, I will keep talking until he snaps and tells me to leave him alone. That would be a welcome change to what's happening right now.

"We can just order in pizza. I'm not really up for going out," he sighs, turning his attention toward the window.

"Don't be ridiculous," I chastise. "We are not going to a city with so many amazing restaurants and eating pizza out of a cardboard box."

"Then pick something, but I don't want to go anywhere stuffy."

"Fair enough. What do you think about Italian? I know a nice, casual place that has an amazing mostaccioli."

"That works." Austin lets go of my hand, reaching behind the seat for a pillow. "I'm going to sleep until we get there. I didn't sleep for shit last night."

"Sounds good." I bring Austin's hand to my lips, kissing each finger. "Remember what I told you. It'll all be okay."

Austin's up and in the shower before I even open my eyes. Today is going to require extra coffee, because every time I fell asleep, his tossing and turning woke me again. Over dinner last night, Austin opened up a bit more and confessed that he's more nervous today than he was when he came out to his family. This time, he feels like it will crush him if his mother pushes him away again. It was foolish of me, but I assured him that won't happen. It can't. If she upsets him, I will step in to protect his heart.

I leave a note on the bed letting Austin know that I am running to Starbucks for a light breakfast and drinks for both of us. He's always slow to get ready in the morning, so I doubt he will even be out of the bedroom before I get back. Even so, I rush down the sidewalk to make sure he's not sitting there alone any longer than he has to be. If he knew how concerned I am he would throw one of his fits where he reminds me that he's not a child and doesn't need me to watch him. Which is amusing because that's one of the few times I'm reminded of how young he is.

"You're a godsend," Austin says dramatically, reaching for the large coffee drink that's so complex it almost embarrasses me to order. "Did you bring back coffee cake, too?"

He reaches for the bag and I hold it high over my head. Had I known he'd be this excited over breakfast pastries, I would have bought everything in the case. I'm caught completely off-guard when Austin jumps on me, wrapping his arms around my neck. "It's not nice to tease someone in my mental state," he scolds.

The bag lowers as Austin kisses his way along my neck, sucking and biting hard enough I start to wonder if I'm going to meet his mother with hickies all over my neck. Then, the little punk swipes the bag out of my hand and jumps down. By the time I get across the room to him, most of the first piece of cake is gone. That's fine by me as long as his face stays bright and worry-free.

Austin changes outfits three times before I pull him away from the suitcase, telling him it's time to go. "Sorry, I just don't want her worrying about me. I know that probably sounds stupid, but--"

"I don't think it's stupid," I assure him. I pull him to my chest, running my fingers through his hair. "It's not your outfit that determines how you're holding up with what they've put you through. I would think the fact that you're staying in school, you have a good job and a stable relationship will be the benchmarks that matter today."

"I know, but you don't understand my family. I swear, my mom would throw out clothes that had a tiny rip or stain when I was younger because my dad would flip his shit because *his family* wouldn't look that way." Austin buries his face in my chest and I smile, knowing that he's sniffing my shirt. It's such a little thing, but it's *his* thing and it's adorable.

"Come on, let's get this over with." I lead him to the door and follow him to the elevator. We're meeting his mother here and then we'll decide what to do for the day. Austin wants to stay here at the hotel, but knowing how upset he is I think it may be wise to go to a park or someplace where they can have some privacy while still being in public.

Austin stiffens as soon as the elevator doors open to the lobby. It takes me all of about five seconds to find his mother, who is an older, feminine version of Austin. "I'm right here. You can do this," I whisper, placing my hand at the small of his back.

"She doesn't look good," he mutters, leaning into my side. "She never looks that tired, David. What if something's wrong?"

There isn't an opportunity to answer him because his mother is rushing our direction. She slows once she's close, her steps faltering more than once.

"Austin, you look amazing," she praises. When she looks at me, I don't see the hate I expected from her. "I'm Sarah. You must be the young man Austin has told me about."

I would laugh at her referring to me as a young man since I'm closer to her age than her son's, but I assume she doesn't know that bit of information. "Yes, ma'am. I'm David. It's nice to meet you."

I step back while she wraps her arms around Austin, sobbing her apologies as she gently rocks him back and forth. And to his credit, Austin relaxes and tells her that it's okay. We all know nothing about the actions of her and her husband is acceptable, but the fact that he's able to put his feelings aside to soothe her says a lot about his character.

The longer they stand there, the more attention they attract, so I suggest that we head out to enjoy the late summer day before it gets too muggy. Austin reaches for my hand, but I motion for him to walk with his mother while I follow. They need this time together and I have no problem being the third wheel.

Chapter Thirteen

Austin

Y ou're father and I are getting a divorce." I trip over my feet when Mom decides to drop this bombshell on me as soon as we're outside the hotel.

"Why?" I ask, assuming this is somehow relevant to why she's reaching out to me now. I should be upset to hear that my parents' marriage is over, but I'm not. I've had a lot of time this week to think about my childhood, and the only conclusion I've drawn is that life would have been much different had this happened when I was little.

I reach out for David's hand, but he shakes his head, choosing to stay behind us. I need him right now, but can't bring myself to say as much, because I still don't trust that my mother is going to accept him as an important part of my life.

"Austin, this has been a long time coming, but once

your sister turned eighteen, I think both of us gave up on trying to make it work." I understand what she's saying, but it doesn't change the fact that I'm pissed off. She may never fully understand just how fucked up our family is because she stayed with his controlling ass because of us. "A few weeks ago, something inside of me snapped. He drove me away from my family over the years, because they couldn't understand why I was with him. He forbade me from talking to you after that night..." She pauses to pull a tissue out of her purse and dabs away the tears in her eyes.

"You'll never know how sorry I am that I let him do that to you. To all of us. He threatened to kick Amanda out if she even mentioned your name. About a month ago, she moved in with Tyler and he told me I couldn't speak to her, either, because she was a little slut."

If I had my own car here, I'd drive to my childhood home and knock the old man on his ass right about now. All of this is because of him. I knew what he was like and tried to bury the pain, but Amanda thought he hung the fucking moon. If at all possible, I hope we can meet up with her before we have to head home because I need to know that she's okay.

We come to the end of the street and I see a bar on one corner and a coffee shop on the other. As much as I'd love a stiff drink, I'm still underage, so I cross the street and hold open the door of the coffee shop for her.

"Everything okay?" David asks as he walks past me. I shake my head, afraid I'll explode if I open my mouth. "Do you want some privacy?"

"Fuck no," I blurt out, reaching for his hand. "Shit's all sorts of fucked up and I need you by me right now. I love you for trying to give us space, but that's only going to make things worse for me."

"Okay." David leads me to the counter, where my mom is already placing her order. David motions to the cashier that we're paying for her drink and she offers him a sad smile. While we're waiting for our turn, David drapes his arms over my shoulders. "What's going on?" he whispers.

"They're getting a divorce. The old man tried pulling the same shit with my little sister as he did with me and she finally hit her breaking point."

"That might be the best thing for everyone." David lowers his voice as my mom joins us. "We'll talk more tonight. Today, let's help your mom make up for lost time."

"Sarah, are you staying in the city tonight?" David asks as we sit down at a small table in the back corner. I kick the side of his foot because there's no fucking way she'll stay down here if she's trying to break free from my father. All of the bank accounts are in his name because he's the one who earned the money. I only know this because the fucker loved to remind her that everything we had was because of him any time they had a disagreement.

"No, I'll be heading back late this evening. I should be okay as long as I'm on the road by ten." She sips her coffee while David tries to convey something to me telepathically. Too bad I have no clue what that message is.

When it becomes apparent that David could stare at me all day and I'd be no closer to understanding him, he turns his attention back to Mom. "Is there any way we could convince you to spend the night? With the school year starting soon, it will be harder for Austin to get up here to see you and I know it would mean a lot to him."

Asshole. Sure, I'm not happy about her leaving to-night, but he's making it sound like my life will be missing something if she leaves me.

"I..." She's trying to figure out how to get out of this gracefully. It can't be easy for her to have gone from spending money without thought to having to budget her dollars.

"Mom, if you don't mind missing church tomorrow morning, I'd like it if you'd stay. You won't need to worry about anything. Maybe we can call Amanda and see if she and Tyler want to join us for dinner," I offer. If she wants to stay, I'll pay for her room and let David pay for ours without fighting with him over it.

"It would be nice to spend time with both of my children." She's considering my offer, which I really didn't think she would.

"Like David said, it'll be tough for me to get up here again before Thanksgiving. And I'd like Amanda to meet David." I'm laying it on thick, but the more I think about it, the more I do want her to stay. I rest my hand on David's thigh and he places his hand over mine.

"That would be nice," she concedes. "I don't know if they'll be able to come down, but I suppose I can call your sister."

"Mom, let me borrow your phone. I'll call her." I hold out my hand, waiting for her to give me what I want. She worries her lip as she pulls the phone out of her purse and hands it to me. I excuse myself from the table to make this call.

I pride myself on being comfortable in any situation, but I find myself looking for any available exit as soon as Austin walks away. I empty my mug and place it on the table with more force than intended.

"Sarah, I don't know exactly what has happened, but you need to understand that I'm trying to look out for your son's best interests. Whether he will say it or not, he needs you right now." Sarah's shoulders slump forward and I can see how much the rift with her son as hurt her. "Whether he will admit it or not, he needs some sort of assurance that you're not going to abandon him again."

"That was never my intention." She looks to the front of the shop, where Austin is having an animated conversation with his sister. "It's no excuse, but I spent twenty-two years playing the role of the good Christian wife. My own parents were older when I was born and I was always taught that the wife is supposed to trust that her husband knows what is best for his family."

"While I can appreciate that, times change. What your husband did to Austin is unforgivable." I sit up straighter, leaning in close enough to lower my voice in case Austin returns. What I'm about to say may be a violation of his trust, but it's necessary. She needs to understand what his life has been like. "When I met Austin, he was sleeping on a concrete slab. He was so ashamed of his standing in life that he spent two months carefully planning every meeting so even I wouldn't know the truth. And I've had to spend every day since then trying to convince him I'm not going to get tired of him and kick him out of my life because your family has taught him to believe love cannot exist without strings."

"That's not true," she responds emphatically. Her posture stiffens now that I've offended her. Good. She needs someone to challenge her beliefs.

"No? Even if you set aside the disgusting fact that you turned your back on him when he finally worked up the courage to tell you the true about his sexual orientation, he's always felt there are standards he had to meet to earn your approval." The barista approaches our table, asking if we'd like refills. I push the mugs to the edge of the table and she retreats, probably to escape the awkward tension between us.

Sarah begins to sob and I hand her a napkin. She dabs at her face before neatly folding the napkin and putting it in her pocket. "I suppose I can see your point. But you have to know, that's all because his father felt certain his career would suffer if we were an ordinary family. Can you help me fix my relationship with my son?"

"I can't make any guarantees, but I will try. The only thing I ask is that you don't toy with his emotions again." Austin returns to the table and Sarah nods her agreement to my conditions. He tells us that his sister won't be able to meet with us until late in the afternoon and that he's asked her to go to their mom's apartment to pick up what she'll need for the night.

He should be happy to be piecing his family back together, but he seems more troubled now than when he excused himself. I push that concern aside for the moment and tuck him close to my side while we continue talking with his mother. She appears uneasy with the simple display of affection, but I won't allow her issues to keep me from giving Austin what he needs.

Austin

My head is killing me by the time we make the short walk back to the hotel. David told me he was going to talk to the front desk about getting Mom into a room of her own and I tried arguing with him, but gave up quickly because it would have required far too much energy to make a strong argument for why he can't keep whipping out his credit cards as if that'll make all of my problems go away. Mom and I sit in the hotel lobby, neither one of us saying anything while we wait for him to return with her room key.

I wonder what she sees when she looks around this place. It's fancier than where most normal families stay, but it's still a far cry from the opulence we're accustomed to. Somehow, I had convinced myself that it was Mom who needed the extravagance, but now I'm beginning to see that she would have been comfortable with the Holiday Inn. She's not the pretentious, materialistic bitch I've made her out to be over the past six months.

David suggests that we relax for a bit and then find somewhere close for lunch, but really, I just want to sleep. I have no fucking clue if it'll be any easier to sleep now that I've seen my mother, but if I don't try, I'm going to be dragging ass later tonight. We step into the elevator and make plans to touch base late this afternoon so we can head to dinner with Amanda and Tyler.

"I'm so proud of you," David whispers as Mom steps off the elevator. "I think all of you need this time together and you're holding up very well."

"Not nearly as well as you think," I admit because

I'm seriously on the verge of a chick-style ugly cry. I feel like I'm mourning the life I never got to have, because my father is a controlling bigot. He's the one who wanted us to look like a Norman Rockwell painting. "I need to shut down for a bit. I'm hoping I'll sleep, but it's doubtful. I just...I never expected any of this. It's a lot to think about."

"That's completely understandable. I'll try to get some work done while you nap since we weren't planning on an entire weekend with the family." Great, now I feel like shit because he's got so much to do before the beginning of the semester. It's really been eye-opening to see how much professors do outside the classroom. Right now, he's working on his first research paper for the university. Apparently, that's a big fucking deal in his world. And he's pushing that aside because of my Jerry Springer family.

I was hoping he'd lie down with me, but I can't ask that of him. Not when he has other shit to do. Now, it's pretty much guaranteed that I won't sleep a single minute.

A soft knock echoes in the back of my mind. Apparently, I was exhausted enough that I did fall asleep. I open my eyes and stretch, just in time to see Amanda sprinting across the room. She dives onto the bed, knocking me flat on my back. "Holy shit, I can't believe you're really here! I didn't even know Mom had your phone number, otherwise I would have made her give it to me," she stays without taking a breath. Her rambling used to annoy the shit out of me, but now it's a sweet melody I could listen to all day. "I tried calling you so many times but your phone wasn't working. I even made Tyler drive down to Madison last month so I could walk around and look for you but you were nowhere to be found."

A month ago? That would have been right about the time I moved in with David. "Sorry, sis. I think Dad blocked my number in your phone so I couldn't call you. And I was so pissed about everything that I didn't think to copy numbers down when I sold my phone." I wrap my arms around her, kissing her long blonde hair. "I missed you, too."

From the sounds of it, David and Tyler are getting along just fine, so I excuse myself long enough to take a leak and throw on a t-shirt. Tyler gives me a manly bro hug, telling me how good I'm looking and I tell him the same. He and I were never best buds, but something's different about him today. I think we're all taking off the masks we were forced to wear for so long. Amanda's moved out to the living area and pats the seat next to her. I flop down and give her a sloppy, wet kiss on the cheek, just to make her squeal in mock disgust.

David and Tyler laugh and excuse themselves, giving us time to catch up. Unlike my reunion with my mom, I'm grateful for the time alone with Amanda. There are questions I want to ask her and things I want to say that I don't need an audience for.

"So, are you really okay with this?" I ask, going for the most important question first. If she has issues with who I am or what I do with my life, there is no point in trying to mend fences.

"Uh, other than the fact that your boyfriend is *way* hotter than mine?" She giggles, fanning herself dramatically. "But if you tell Tyler I said that, I will so deny it."

"So you really don't have a problem with me liking

guys?" I push, not satisfied with her answer. I need to hear her tell me that my sexuality won't be a thing between us.

"No, you idiot! I know what Dad said to you, but I'm not like him. Much to his chagrin, you're not the first gay person I know. And honestly, I kind of wondered about you a few times, but didn't dare bring it up because I didn't want to upset you." Amanda crawls into my lap, the way she did when she was little. "You need to cut mom some slack, too. She's pretty messed up over everything and she's convinced you hate her."

"I don't hate her. Fuck, I don't even know if I hate Dad. He's an asshole, but I think hating him requires way more emotional energy than he's worth. I'm just thankful she called me and we can figure out where to go from here."

"It sucks that you're so far away," Amanda whines. "I'm going to U of M this fall because that's where Tyler's at and you'll be all the way in Madison. Will you promise to come home for Thanksgiving and Christmas? And call at least once a week? And not ignore me if I text you?"

"Getting awfully pushy now that you're an adult, aren't you?" I tease. Truthfully, I love that she's so adamant about keeping in touch, because now that I have part of my family back, I don't want to lose them again.

"Austin, you have to promise me. Seriously, I know we were at each other's throats a lot over the past few years, but not being able to bug the crap out of you sucks." She bats her big hazel eyes at me, as if that's going to have some sort of effect. Then again, those doe eyes have gotten her just about everything she wants for most of her life, so I doubt she even realizes she's doing it. When her lower lip sticks out in a pathetic pout, I push her off the couch roaring with laughter as she squeals. "You're an asshole! I take it all back!"

I reach out to her, helping her off the ground. "You love me and you know it. Yes, I solemnly swear I will never ignore you. Unless, of course, I'm busy with my hotter than hell boyfriend, in which case it might take a few hours."

"I seriously don't know whether I should be grossed out or jealous after that comment," she teases. "Come on, we'd better get going before Mom comes looking for us."

Sitting in the hotel lounge with Tyler has been eye opening to say the very least. I have been given few glimpses into Austin's past and feel like I am treading in rough seas whenever I try to broach the subject with him. Sadly, I've learned more about Austin's childhood in the past thirty minutes than the past few months.

The picture Tyler has painted of Austin and Amanda's father is depressing. While they have never suffered physical mistreatment, they were subjected to veiled emotional abuse from the time they were young children. Yes, that sounds extreme, but there's no other way to put it.

If they put their all into a task or activity, their father wanted to know why they didn't do more. Their impressionable minds were filled with elitist principles about how families in certain income brackets should behave, including the fact that they shouldn't socialize with those less fortunate. Every cell in Tyler's body seized as he told me about all the times he was forced to listen to Amanda's father tell her that Tyler would never amount to anything because of the neighborhood his family lived in. I feel an odd sense of pride for this virtual stranger because he's obviously making strides to prove the old man wrong. I understand how that can fuel a young man to succeed, because I was much the same way.

Tyler and I slide off our stools when Sarah, Austin, and Amanda walk through the entry to the lounge. I slide one hand to the small of Austin's back while pulling out a high-backed stool for his mother. He leans into me, whispering thanks for my part in making this happen. I didn't do this, all I did was pull out my credit card. And I'd pay many times what I've spent for the opportunity to see three members of this family trying to heal the wounds carved over the past twenty years.

I quickly become the outsider of the group as the others try to catch up on everything that's been going on in their lives since the night Austin was unceremoniously dropped at the bus stop and told to not return. My jaw begins to hurt from grinding my teeth because I can't stop imagining what it would be like to tell Dennis Pritchard what I think of his self-righteous attitude. His pride and need for acceptance has cost him the one thing most people would hold onto above all else: a beautiful wife and two amazing children.

Before long, Austin notices my discomfort and suggests that we find someplace to eat. When it was going to be three of us, I was going to take Austin and his mother to a steakhouse one of my colleagues raved about after a trip up here, so I defer to those who are more familiar with the area. The four of them wind up debating which restaurant to go to and Austin wins out by suggesting that we go to a Woodfire Grill close by. His mother's tightly crossed arms and pursed lips tell me that she's less than thrilled with the chosen venue, but she politely follows her children through the lobby and down the street. The more time I spend with her, the more I wonder if she's lost the ability to voice her own opinions.

"If you would prefer we don't go there, all you have to do is say the word," I whisper, hanging back to walk beside Sarah.

"It's fine," she responds flatly. "Austin used to love going there when we came to the city and tonight is about him."

It's early enough that we don't have to wait long for a table. Sarah peruses the wine list and then slides it across the table. When our waiter arrives, I ask if she'd like to share a bottle and she declines even though her eyes seem glued to that leather binder. I pick it up and choose a bottle of Merlot, hoping she will start to loosen up if she has a glass. I highly doubt it will take more than that.

Sarah offers me a meek smile over the rim of her glass and I nod, letting her know I understand. I don't, not really, because I can't imagine anyone allowing their spirit to be dimmed as much as she has over the years or the notion that a man could do this to the woman he loves.

Everything goes well all the way through dinner. The tension from earlier in the night has evaporated and it seems the Pritchard clan is well on their way to healing. And then, no sooner than I allow that thought to cross my mind, everyone at the table becomes still as statues. I stare at Austin, watching as his eyes dart around the restaurant, terrified.

I flag the waiter over, still clueless as to what has

caused the drastic shift in the mood and hand him my credit card without asking to see the bill. I need to get them out of here because something has them spooked.

"Why don't we head back to the hotel?" I suggest. I'm not a man who deals well with feeling helpless, which is exactly what I am right now. "If you would like, everyone can come up to our room for a while so you can keep talking."

Austin mouths the words thank you as he springs from his chair and makes one last pass of the room before locking his gaze somewhere near the front of the building. No longer willing to be kept in the dark, I make my way around the table and wrap an arm around his waist. "What is going on? I get the impression it's something bad, but I'm a bit out of my element here."

"Over there," Austin whispers back, nodding his head to where he's still staring. His chest rises and falls rapidly while he repeatedly clenches his fists. "Out of all the fucking restaurants in this fucking state, it figures he couldn't give me one night to be normal."

Austin is staring at a portly older gentleman with a younger brunette leaning in, running her manicured fingers over his arm. "I don't mean to seem dense, but you need to give me a little bit more." I hate making the request, but there are many ways this could be headed.

As though he could tell we were talking about him, the man turns his head and he freezes in place, the same way everyone else did. This night has gone from a blessing to a curse in under a minute. I watch him lean in to whisper something to his date, who immediately excuses herself to the bathroom. Amanda takes a step in that direction and I reach out to stop her. Whoever that is, nothing good will come from causing a scene.

"Amanda, let's get out of here," I suggest, hoping she doesn't think I'm trying to control her. It takes a moment, but her posture softens and she nods slightly. "Austin, explain," I demand quietly.

"Leave it to dear ol' dad to fuck up what seemed to be a good night." Austin reaches for my hand, squeezing to the point of pain as we make our way to the entrance. I'm not sure how I'm able to make it to the hostess stand to collect my credit card without running into everyone, because I'm now obsessed with watching the man I have had more than one violent fantasy about today.

"Austin," an authoritative voice calls out as we're walking back to the hotel. Despite the fact that Austin is several inches shorter than I am, I find myself nearly jogging to keep up to his pace. Tyler tucks Amanda close to his side and reaches for Sarah's hand. "You were raised better than to ignore me when I'm speaking to you, boy."

Something inside Austin snaps and he drops my hand as he turns to confront his father. Tyler looks over his shoulder and I motion for them to continue to the hotel. I'm going to do my best to defuse the situation and that will be easier if I only have to deal with two stubborn men and not the addition of two angry women and a protective boyfriend.

"Austin, don't do anything you will regret," I warn him. His father has already drawn the attention of several people on the street and no matter what this man has coming to him, it isn't worth Austin damaging his future.

"Go back to the hotel, David. I have some things I

have to say to him and I don't want you to hear them."

"That is precisely why I won't leave you here alone with him. If you can't say it in front of me, think long and hard about whether it's worth saying at all."

"How cute," the old man sneers, stepping into Austin's personal space. "Tell me, did you rush back to school and find yourself a new daddy as soon as you got off the bus or did it take you a while to realize that you're incapable of anything without a strong man telling you what to do."

I push Austin behind me, keeping him out of his father's reach. It's obvious he's been drinking and isn't any more happy to see his family than they were to see him. That may have something to do with the girl who can't be much older than Austin who's sitting on a park bench at the other end of the block.

"Sir, if you can't speak to Austin with respect, this conversation is finished," I warn him. Austin tugs at the back of my shirt, hissing at me to stop. I can't do that because I refuse to let this man, and I use that term lightly, cause the man I love any additional pain.

"Respect?" Mr. Pritchard cackles. "Boy, you're really something, sticking your nose where it doesn't belong. You have no right to tell me what I can or cannot do when it comes to my son."

"I disagree," I retort. Austin steps to my side, pleading with me to stop. "You lost the right to expect anything from Austin the moment you decided you were through with him because he refused to conform to your delusional standards of what he should be."

"While it's obvious that you are likely closer to my age than my son's, I'm assuming you don't have children, correct?" I nod, unsure why I am giving him the satisfaction of sitting here listening to him. Somehow, I hope that it will help the rest of the family if I allow him to verbally beat on me. Perhaps he will be able to release his anger and eventually salvage some sort of relationship with his children.

"I didn't think so. Then you know nothing about what it's like for a father to be forced to the point of turning his back on his only son, because the boy simply refuses to place a higher priority on morality than his own sick and twisted desires."

I swallow hard, fighting the urge to lash out at him. *I'm doing this for Austin and Amanda,* I remind myself while he continues ranting. I'm no longer listening to what he's saying because it's nothing that will sway my opinion in the least.

"You self-centered son of a bitch," Austin screams as he lunges at his father. I'm able to pull him back before he is able to do any real damage, and hopefully before anyone can call the police for this debacle. "You sit there and preach about the difference between right and wrong, and yet you're the one sitting in there having a cozy dinner with our old fucking babysitter!" *Well, that explains a lot.* "Tell me, do you really think any of us are stupid enough to think that you waited until after Mom moved out before you started fucking her?"

"Don't you take that tone of voice with me," Austin's father sneers. He raises his hand and I release Austin, suddenly wishing Tyler had sent the women on their way and stayed with us. There is no way I am going to be able to keep them from pummeling one another into the pavement for much longer.

"I believe we're done here. Austin gave you a chance to say what you wanted to say, but it's obvious that you haven't learned a thing in the months since you last saw him." Austin's still ready to snap so I tighten my grip on his hand. "No matter how much you would like to think he will fail without you, I have to believe you did him a favor by cutting him out of your life. He's been forced to find a way to survive without your support and he's stronger for it. It's a shame, really, because you will never see what an amazing man your son is."

"You want him? Keep him because it's obvious he has no intention of changing his life or doing the right thing." Austin winces at the words, shrinking at hearing his father once again turning his back on his flesh and blood.

Austin's father spits on the ground near his son's feet and turns to walk away. I don't bother telling Austin how much better off he is without that asshole in his life or how much more I respect him for becoming the man he is in spite of his father's hateful influence because he won't believe me right now. He's a wounded child, struggling to come to terms with everything that's been said.

Austin

The only thing worse than having to hear how much I disgust my father is having to hear it again, this time in front of David. I sink into David's side and allow him to guide me back to the hotel. Eventually, I'll go through the full spectrum of emotions again, but right now, I'm just fucking numb.

"You can't let his words get to you," David says as he slides the keycard into the lock. He holds the door for me and I enter without acknowledging him and head directly for the bedroom. I need to get out of these clothes because it's the only thing I can do right now to distance myself from that clusterfuck.

I need to check on my mom. No way in hell did she know that my father hadn't been faithful to her. If she had, she wouldn't have looked like she'd just been stabbed when she saw him sitting with Lisa. As if it's not bad enough that he couldn't keep from slipping his dick where it didn't belong, he did it with someone we've known since she was just a kid.

"Austin, say something," David pleads. I shrug away when he places a hand on my shoulder. I can't have him close to me right now. As much as I want to fall into his arms and cry, I can't because I can't rely on him to save me. Unfortunately, David doesn't seem to understand where my heads at and he closes his hand around my wrist, refusing to let me go. "Don't do this. You can't let him get to you that way."

"You think I don't know that?" I scream, jerking my arm, trying to get away. "Too bad it's not that easy. And believe it or not, I really don't give a shit about what he said about me. It's nothing I haven't heard before. I want to kill him for what he did to Mom."

David's chest presses against my back as he kisses the side of my neck. I tilt my head to the side, no longer capable of fighting myself over what I need right now. "Let me help you. Let me take care of you tonight and prove just how wrong he is. You're none of the things he says you are and I know that because I could never be this hopelessly in love with you if you were."

"I told you, it's not about that," I argue. "I need to see how my mom's doing. I need to call her."

"Amanda and Tyler are probably with her. Let them take care of her while I help you," he insists. He's right, as always, but how can I let him take away my pain by way of a mind-blowing orgasm while my family is two floors beneath us suffering? "Let's go take a shower and try to relax. Then, we'll head to your mom's room and you'll see that I'm right."

"Okay," I relent. David turns me in his arms, reaching down with one hand to release the button on my pants before sliding them over my hips. I moan when his fingers trail through the cleft of my ass, taunting me, making promises of what's to come.

The bathroom quickly fills with steam while David works to strip both of us. I allow him to take my hand and lead me into the walk-in shower, suddenly wishing we were home so we had more room to move around. While there is something to be said for being forced to stay in close proximity, I've learned to appreciate the way David makes use of every single shower-head in our master bathroom.

"You are a beautiful, driven man, Austin," David praises as he pushes me under the stream of water. I watch as he reaches for the body wash, feel him as he presses his thickening cock into the cleft of my ass. I bite on my lip to keep from begging him to take me. I want the pain to remind me of my place in the world because right about now, I'm struggling to believe that he won't leave me. I *need* those silent promises.

His slick hands knead my shoulders before traveling lower to pinch both of my nipples at the same time. I moan, leaning back to allow him to hold me upright. "If I have to, I will remind you every day of every reason I have fallen in love with you. One of these days, you are going to realize I have no plans to leave you. I am far too busy to waste my time with passing flings. I look forward to teaching you what it truly means to love and be loved unconditionally."

"I want that, David. I want you to teach me because I don't like being this person," I mutter sadly. I'm still unsure whether or not it's possible to change everything that's been ingrained in me throughout my life, but if it is, I want David to be the one to help me turn my thinking around.

David's hand grips my jaw, forcing me to look at him. When our eyes meet, I shrink back into myself because I can't stand the anger I see in his eyes. "It's. Not. Your Fault."

"I know that, but it doesn't change the fact that you deserve someone who isn't so unbelievably fucked up. I don't want you to wake up one day and decide that you're at a point in your life where you don't feel like dealing with my daddy issues anymore."

"That will never happen," he promises me. His hands massage my ass, holding me while he gently rocks his hips, grinding his cock into my stomach. "And while I'm not a violent man, I assure you that will change if you insist on trying to make me believe the lies you tell yourself about the type of man you are."

I suck in a sharp breath at the thought of David's strong hands landing on my bare ass. It's not my thing, but now there's something appealing about the concept. "Okay," I moan because it's the only word I can come up with. David's doing a damn good job making me forget the world beyond this small room. He slides one finger through my crease, nudging at my hole. I push back, desperate to have him take me.

"Not yet," he scolds. He takes his sweet ass time trailing his hands over my ass and hips, coming close to giving me what I want more than anything right now, but repeatedly moves away just when I think he's going to give in.

"David, please," I finally beg, no longer giving a damn how pathetic I sound.

"Put your hands on the wall," he instructs me. His

voice is easily a full octave lower than normal and that low timbre sends a jolt straight to my dick, bringing me embarrassingly close to release. "I will *always* give you everything you need. You have to trust that."

His affirmations continue as he plunges a slick finger deep inside my body, curling until he finds the sweet spot that always short circuits my brain. I'm reduced to incoherent babbling by the time he adds a second finger, scissoring them to stretch me. I feel the hot head of his cock separating me, taunting me even more. "Then do it," I urge desperately.

With one hand on the middle of my back, David guides his cock to my entrance. With agonizing tenderness, he enters me, the entire time whispering promises for the future. Even in my lusty haze, I'm not sure I fully believe them, but for the moment, I give in to the picture he's painting for us.

Chapter Fifteen

David

For a brief moment, I allowed myself to believe that Austin wouldn't allow his father's words and actions to affect him. Logically, I know that's nearly impossible because he has spent so much of his life working to please his father, but I was hoping the love we share would be enough.

After showing him how much he means to me, the two of us dressed and spent the rest of the evening with what's left of his family. They pressed Austin to tell them everything that happened after they left us on the sidewalk with Mr. Pritchard. He did, and they all assured him that his father's thoughts are not the opinions of the entire family. This morning, we all met in the hotel restaurant for brunch before saying good-bye. The original plan was to spend another day together, but I don't think any of them can pretend to be a happy family right now. So, we parted ways with promises for them to visit us in Wisconsin soon and his mother planning on a family Christmas without any drama.

"Do you want to talk about it?" I ask. With every mile we travel, Austin has slunk deeper in his seat closing in on himself.

"Nope."

I place my hand on his knee, debating whether I should push him to let it out or give him time. He shifts in his seat so both knees are pressed close to the door. At the rate he's going, I wouldn't be surprised if he tries to sit in the back seat once we stop for gas. I know better than to assume I have done something to upset him, but that makes it that much harder to deal with the growing chasm between us.

It's not until after Austin falls asleep with his head pressed to the window that I attempt to touch him again. This is the first time since we've met that I've questioned whether or not I am a fool for thinking we can have a healthy, satisfying relationship. If I'm the man who's realizing too late in life what he wants. If Chad was right and I'm setting myself up for heartache when Austin decides he wants to run around and do the things most kids his age are doing.

With one hand on the wheel, I brush a messy curl away from Austin's forehead. With his hair grown out a bit, he looks even younger, more innocent. I can't help but keep running that one lock of hair between my fingers as I drive, trying to hold onto the connection I once thought was strong but now doubt.

"Baby, we're home," I whisper as I pull the car into the garage. He stirs, barely opening his eyes to look at me. And for that brief moment when he's drifting between sleep and waking, he forgets everything that's weighing on his mind and leans into my touch. I close the distance between us, kissing him with tender desperation, pleading with my lips for him to believe me this time.

And then it ends. Austin pulls away from me and gets out of the car without a word. I watch him walk into the house, wondering how we got so incredibly off-track this weekend. I shake off the terrifying thought that this is the beginning of the end and head into the house, listening for sounds from upstairs as I start a load of laundry and rummage through the kitchen trying to figure out what to make for dinner.

The silent treatment continues throughout the night. It's not until after dinner that I notice the backpack sitting next to the front door. At that point, it becomes impossible to ignore what is happening between us. "Austin, is there something you need to tell me?" I ask, not sure I want to hear his answer.

"What are you talking about?" he responds.

"I don't know, perhaps the fact that your backpack that hasn't been out of the closet since we moved in is now sitting by the front door." I take a few breaths because I'm perilously close to losing my temper and I know that won't do either of us any good. "If something has you upset, you need to find a way to talk about it. It seems to me that you are convinced I'm going to decide you are unworthy of my affections and you're trying to leave before I make that decision."

"It's not that," Austin mumbles. His gaze is fixed on the barely touched plate in front of him and I want to reach up and force him to look at me.

"No?" I challenge, crossing my arms tightly across my chest as I lean back in my chair. "Then perhaps you can tell me what it is because I'm in the dark here."

To his credit, Austin doesn't kick the chair out of

his way and run for the door the way he would have a few months ago if faced with this situation. He is learning, albeit slowly, how to communicate rather than run. Instead, he picks up his fork, suddenly ravenously hungry. Every time his mouth is empty, he quickly refills it so he won't have to speak to me. Finally, I reach across the table, yanking the fork out of his hand and scooping up the rest of his silverware.

"Austin, if you don't tell me what I'm doing wrong, I can't make it right. I told you when we first got together that I don't have much more experience than you when it comes to relationships. The difference is, I'm willing to work at this one to build something with you."

"You're not doing anything wrong," he assures me. "Well, that's not exactly true, but I don't think you mean to do it."

"Do what?" I ask, growing agitated. I move to the chair next to Austin, reaching out to hold his hand. "This is what I'm talking about. If you don't know if I'm messing up as far as you're concerned, then how am I supposed to know? And furthermore, how am I supposed to stop doing whatever it is that I may or may not be doing?"

Austin lets his head fall back, pinching the bridge of his nose with his free hand. Beneath the table, I can feel his leg bouncing with pent up nerves. "Like I said, it's not you. It's me. I should be fucking thrilled that you want to take care of me and protect me, but it does nothing but make me feel weak and pathetic. It's like you don't think I'm capable of dealing with my shit on my own and you have to jump in to do it for me.

"And this weekend you did it in front of my father. The man already thinks I'm worthless because I like dick, but now he knows that I need a man to hold me up when dealing with all the bullshit."

"Is that how you see it?" I ask, moving my hand up his arm and around to the back of his neck. "I'm sorry if you feel that way, but I also don't know if it's something I can change. I have never been the type of person who can let someone else get hurt and not want to do something to help. It's not a sign of weakness on your part. It's quite the opposite in fact; you're an incredibly strong and capable man, but you've been taking on too much for too long. This is the first time you've had someone who can and will relieve some of that burden for you. Even the strongest people in the world need to take a break sometimes."

"That's great, but what about everyone else? Seriously, it's awesome that you want to take my shit on as your own, but that doesn't change the fact that my father will *never* respect me after the way you rode in on your white horse."

He tries to get up, but I hold firm to the back of his neck and pull him closer for a kiss. If we are going to keep this discussion alive, we need to move to another room. Preferably one where I can wrap both arms around him and hold tight because he may not like what I have to say.

I lead him to the living room, pulling him into the oversized chair that I thought was ridiculous when Becky suggested it, but now love to sit in because it's the perfect size for both of us. Once my arms are containing him, I steady myself to deliver the hard truth that he already knows but doesn't want to admit.

"Austin, there is nothing you can do that will force your father to respect you. Even before this weekend, he strikes me as the type of man who wouldn't care if you won the Nobel Peace Prize because you aren't living your life according to the blueprints her drew up for creating a legacy. If you crawled to him on your hands and knees apologizing and telling him that you aren't really gay, he'd kick you to the ground for being foolish enough to even think that you were." Rather than fight with me, Austin turns in the chair, curling up with his head on my shoulder. I know this is painful for him to hear, but the sooner we get past this point in his life, the sooner the healing can begin.

"Your father is a bully and a control freak. I realized that before even seeing the way he treated you Saturday night. It's obvious in the way your mother carries herself, as if she can't trust her own thoughts anymore. She might never forgive herself for letting your father forbid her from talking to you." I run my fingers through his hair, turning his face to mine so I can get a read on whether or not I'm going too far for one night. Oddly, he seems more content now than he has all weekend.

"Instead of using him as an excuse to leave, you need to realize how many people love you and support you. Those who truly matter will be happy that you have someone in your life who is willing to stand beside you no matter what happens."

"I know, I just--"

"No!" I press my finger to his lips to keep him from rambling. It's not that I don't want him to have a voice; it's simply that I can't handle hearing the justifications running through his mind right now. "You are going to drive yourself mad if you keep creating reasons why you can't be happy. You *can be* and you deserve to be. Now, if you don't mind, I think it's time to go to bed because we both have a long day tomorrow."

"Huh?" He looks at me, confused and utterly adorable.

"I have to work and you have to get your books. Before you know it, our lazy summer will be over and we will probably be too tired by the end of the day to do anything fun."

"Speak for yourself, old man," Austin teases. "First of all, this has probably been the busiest summer of my life, the first one where I didn't sit on my ass waiting for the next school year to begin."

"I know, baby. And I'm proud of you for working hard enough that you are still going to school full-time."

"And I don't have to worry about what happens after school starts because I'm young enough that it won't kill me to live on a few hours of sleep during the week when it's necessary. I'll just tuck you into bed at eight-thirty so your weary bones can get some rest and then go into the office to get my shit done." I pinch his backside as punishment for teasing me even though it's probably the best outcome I could have hoped for tonight.

On the way to the bedroom, I grab his backpack, dumping the contents on our bed before making a grand show of burying the canvas bag at the back of the closet.

Austin

Over five-hundred dollars later, I think I'm ready for school. David offered me the keys to the car so I could take everything back to the house and relax until he's done, but I, in my infinite wisdom, told him I would be fine hanging out on my own until he's ready. Now, I'm hunched over and feeling sympathy for pack mules in the mountains because it sucks ass walking uphill with this much weight on my back.

It's been a while since I've been able to spend time with Bree and Casey and I'm hoping to rectify that today. There are times I get the impression Casey thinks I somehow took the easy way out by moving in with David. At least, I hope that's the reason he's been more distant the past couple of times we've talked, because the only other issue I can think of is the fact that I'm gay. Sure, Bree told me that he had an issue in the past with someone making unwanted passes at him, but I'd like to think he's not so narrow-minded that he'd paint every gay person with the same brush.

"Austin!" I drop my bag to the ground and turn around just in time to see Bree running up behind me. She throws her arms over my shoulders and hugs me tightly. "You look amazing! You wanna head to my place and you can tell me all about how the good life is treating ya?"

The good life. That's a joke. Sure, I'm no longer on the streets, but in some ways, I think that short time of my life was easier than all the bullshit I'm dealing with now. It sucked not knowing where my food was coming from or where I would sleep from one night to the next, but I quickly stripped myself of the self-conscious insecurities that keep me up part of every single night now. I was living for myself and didn't give a shit what anyone thought of me. I was already at rock bottom, so I never pondered what would happen to me if the rug was yanked out from beneath me.

The best thing about running into Bree while Casey is off doing some day labor is that I can get rid of this damn bag of books and other random shit. Just to be safe, I carefully set the bag on the floor because it wouldn't surprise me if the load is too much for the rundown building's floor to hold with any sort of impact.

Funny, at the beginning of summer, I thought this place was practically a palace. It was a safe harbor when I otherwise had none, a place for me to hold onto the last shreds of my dignity and maintain the lie for as long as I did. Now that I'm getting back on my feet, I realize just how crappy this little place is. But it's Bree's, so I would never voice that opinion.

"Sit and I'll grab something to drink." I look over my shoulder as Bree straightens up in the kitchen area of the apartment, noticing that it's much better stocked now than it used to be. It makes me wonder how things are going in her relationship because her resolve to live a transient lifestyle for the sake of love seems to be waning. "So, tell me what's going on with you and the sexy professor."

I'm uncomfortable every time I think about the fact that he's a professor at the university. Everyone tells me it's not that big of a deal and that we aren't the only couple with a student/faculty relationship, but I'd bet most of the other couples don't have such a wide age gap between them. They also aren't in the position where the student has to completely rethink their career path because there's no way I'll be able to get through the program without having David as an instructor.

"Oh, get that look off your face. I thought you were getting over all the stupidity over why you shouldn't be with him and just, as you put it, doing what feels right for once in your life." She smacks the back of my head before hurdling over the top of the couch, landing close enough I have to move my drink quickly to keep from dumping it all over. "You have a gorgeous man who loves you, a house most people your age would kill to live in, and you know he supports you no matter what you do. There is no reason whatsoever for those creases in your forehead."

"Yeah, but it's not as easy as it seems," I admit. "Sometimes, I think I'd be better off back down here with the two of you."

"Fuck that noise! You know the deal with me and Casey, so you know I'm more qualified than most to call your ass out this time," she scolds. That's not what I expected. If anything, I thought she would be the one person in the world who can understand where I'm coming from. "If you were still out there with us every night, it would cause a whole host of issues for the two of you."

"But at least then I would know my place in the world," I mumble, quickly taking a drink to mask how hard this shit is for me to admit.

"Again, I say that's total shit. I'm starting to think you've spent too much time with Casey," she criticizes. "He has a comfortable, albeit dumpy, place to stay, but he lets his pride and doubt get in the way. He thinks that living in the apartment that my parents help me pay for proves that he's incapable of taking care of himself. He also worries that he can't get comfortable here because I'll get sick of supporting him and dump him back out on the streets. What he fails to realize, and what I hope you *do see* is that by being so stubborn, he's driving a wedge between us."

"Are things not going well?" I ask, hating that she no longer gets the little sparkle in her eyes when she talks about him. When I first met them, I thought of them as a couple that could conquer whatever life threw at them.

"Depends." Bree gets up and starts dusting the furniture to keep me at a distance.

"On? Come on, I know we haven't known one another long, but you need to take a bit of your advice. Let me in." I walk across the room and pull the static duster out of her hand, holding her in place so she can't escape. Oh, the irony of being the one trying to get someone to listen. "You listened to me bitch and complain often enough, now it's your turn to vent before you blow."

We settle back on the couch and she explains what's going on between her and the man she loves. From the sounds of it, it all boils down to the fact that she doesn't want to keep playing the role of a homeless girl once school starts. She wants to be able to come back to her crappy apartment and do her schoolwork like a normal person. She doesn't want to have to worry about explaining why she's homeless but not to her classmates. Basically, she wants everything I have the chance to have and I'm sitting here bitching about it.

"So, what are you going to do?" I ask her when she tells me that it's been causing almost daily fights between the couple.

"I'm giving him until the first snowfall to get his head out of his ass," she says bluntly. "And I've told him that once school starts I'm coming here to do what I need to do and then I'll meet him down at the park. I really don't want to even do that, but it's the most I'm willing to bend. I've worked too hard to let him screw this up for me."

"Makes sense," I agree.

By the time David calls to find out where I'm at, I'm feeling better than I thought possible about living with David. Our situations aren't the same, but no way in hell would I want to be in either Bree or Casey's spot. Now, I have to figure out how to make sure David knows that my head is no longer firmly shoved up my own ass.

Chapter Sixteen

Austin

C had wants us to come over tonight. He has a
proposition for you," David informs me as he
waits for a break in traffic so we can head home.
Home. After spending most of the day with Bree, that
simple four-letter word has new meaning. She made
me realize that it's not the structure, but the feeling I
have when I'm with the man to my left.

The entire way down State Street, I tried to come
up with a way to show David that I'm done letting fear
ruin my life. He's told me more than once that the
best way I can get back at my father for being such a
miserable fuck is to live my life and be happy. Starting
right now, that's my plan. I'm going to bust my ass to
get the best grades I can and go home at the end of the
day to the man who's taught me what it means to love.

"Hey, you in there?" David asks, breaking me from
my thoughts. He runs his fingers through my hair,
tugging gently to hold my attention.

"Sorry, just thinking about some shit," I tell him. When I turn to face him, I swear I just about melt into a pile of goo right in my seat. He's always sexy, but the softness in his eyes is what does me in. The way his amusement shows through the slight upturn of his mouth. "I'm cool with heading over there for a while, but I'll admit I was hoping to spend a nice, low-key night at home."

"We won't stay long," he promises me. "He thinks he has a way to keep you working for him during school without burning yourself out. I know you don't want me meddling, but I won't lie and tell you that's not part of what led to this idea. I know you feel like you need to work so you can support yourself, and while I respect that I also know how hard it will be for you to maintain your grades while working as much as possible."

The fact that David's started rambling more often lately is a sign of how off-center my shit has made him. When we first met, he was this take-charge guy who knew exactly what he wanted in life. Now, he's sitting there apologizing and explaining his actions before I even get upset, which I'm not about to because I know he did this because he loves me. Unlike the man I've wasted so much time worrying about pleasing, David loves me for me and will do whatever he can to make sure I'm happy. That right there is pretty fucking awesome.

"David, I think my bad habits are starting to rub off on you." I laugh, leaning over to kiss his cheek. "Thank you. I'm not upset."

"You're not?" he asks, disbelief heavy in his voice.

"No. I get that you are trying to help me do what I need to so I don't kill myself within the first month. I know I've given you a lot of shit about how I don't

want you to support me, and I still don't, but I've realized that there are other ways I can contribute to the
house and part of that is staying focused so you won't
always have to pay for me." He pulls into a parking lot
and turns in his seat as soon as the car is stopped.
His slack jaw would be amusing if not for how hard
I've fought him every step of the way.

"Even though I suck at proving it, I love you and I
am so blessed to have found you when I did," I continue. Pretty soon, I'm sure the sappy instrumental music will start playing in the background, but whatever.
This is shit I wouldn't have to say if I wasn't such an
idiot most of the time. "You saved me when I didn't
want to be. And ever since then, you have taught me
what it's like to be loved. You've made me see that
I *deserve* to be with someone as amazing as you. It
wasn't until today that I realized just how much I was
hurting you by trying to prove my independence."

"Wow. That's...wow." I chuckle at the fact that I
have, quite possibly for the first time since we met,
rendered David speechless. He pulls me over the console of the small car so the gearshift is pressing uncomfortably into my leg. "I love you, too, babe. I don't
want to sound ungrateful or anything after that beautiful speech, but what caused the change of heart? I
was certain you would be upset with me for at least a
few days."

Before I can answer, David kisses me deeply, devouring my mouth as he slides his hand beneath the
waistband of my shorts. The man who's usually all
about propriety and not doing anything the slightest
bit indecent in public is about two seconds away from
stripping me right here and fucking me in the car. I
place my hands on the center of David's chest, pushing away from him even though it's the last fucking

thing I want.

"If I knew you'd react that way, I might have talked to Bree sooner." I laugh, straightening the front of David's shirt so it doesn't look like we've been making out like a couple of teenagers. Shit, I must be getting old if I'm thinking that way. Either that or David's having a good influence on me.

"Remind me to buy her something great to say thank you," he sighs, leaning his head against the headrest for a moment. I swear he looks more relaxed than he has in a while. "Okay, what do you say we head to Chad's for a bit and then bow out as soon as possible? I'm suddenly not feeling terribly sociable."

David

Every time I think I have Austin figured out, the man surprises me. I knew it was risky to go behind his back to ask Chad to find an office job for him, but I had to do it. It was either that or say something about the course load he's taking on this coming semester, and I knew that would be relationship suicide.

"So, you suddenly have the need for someone willing to work from home with a flexible schedule to take care of your billing?" I ask smugly when Chad and I wind up on the deck with beers in hand as is becoming the routine every time we visit. As usual, Austin is inside with Becky, helping in the kitchen and playing with the baby. I used to worry that he was trying to give us a wide berth, but now I see that he and Becky have grown quite close. It's an interesting dynamic that seems to work for our group.

"Well, ya know..." Chad smirks from behind the

longneck bottle. "I figured it works for all of us. He can work around his schedule, I don't have to deal with that shit, and you won't rag my ass if he's not home at a decent hour."

"Does that mean you're thawing a bit when it comes to the idea of the two of us together?" Perhaps it is a bit hypocritical that I am so obsessed with gaining Chad's acceptance while telling Austin he needs to stop worrying about what others think of him or us, but I see it as two completely unique situations. Chad is essentially a part of our day-to-day lives given the fact that he's my best friend and Austin's boss, so I feel compelled to know what he truly feels about Austin as my partner before it creates a strain on any of the individual relationships.

"Yeah, it's obvious you two are stupid in love and he's a good guy. I was worried at first, but the number of times you've called me bitching about how he won't let you carry him through life proves that I was wrong." Chad hands me another bottle and I wonder if he is hoping to get me tipsy again tonight. I hope not, because he will be disappointed because my only plan is to get Austin home and curl up next to him in the bed.

"It's nice to see that you are man enough to admit it," I chide. I look at the setting sun, realizing that I have the life I have spent so many years working toward; my dream job, a house I helped design and build, topped off with a man that I could see myself growing old with. All of that combined with a small core of amazing friends makes every struggle I faced in my own childhood worthwhile because I know enough to appreciate what I have been given. "I seem to have him broken of the idea that me caring for him is the same as me keeping him from drowning, so that's a start. I thought he would be livid when I told him that we talked about him working in your office, but he shocked the hell out of me by going into this long speech about how he's done fighting me."

"That's good for both of you. I think the two of you are good for each other. I was beginning to think you were going to turn into some crazy old man on the porch yelling at kids to get off the lawn."

"I still might," I say drily. "It's a nice lawn. I hate to cut this short, but I need to get back on a decent schedule, otherwise there's no way I'll survive the first week of school."

"Better watch it, otherwise you're going to start eating dinner at four-thirty and tucking in for the night before eight, old man." Chad doubles over laughing at his own joke. Sadly, before this summer he may not have been too far from the truth. Luckily, I have Austin around to keep me young. "Go, but don't forget the two of you are coming up to the cabin for Labor Day if I don't see you before then."

"Sounds good." Chad follows me into the house and pulls Austin aside to give him some information for his new job before walking us to the door.

I want to talk to Austin on the way home to find out his honest thoughts about the job opportunity, but it seems pointless given the fact that he's using his cell phone as a light so he can see the thick packet of information he received from Chad. I'm impressed with the fact that he's diving right in, but part of me wonders if it's still too much. Yes, he will be working from home, but that doesn't negate the fact that it is a lot to take on. One of the many things I have learned about Austin since we met is that he attempts to give his all to everything he does. That has worked fine over the summer, but we will have to see how it goes once he is a few weeks into the school year.

"Are you all set for next week or do you need to do some shopping yet this week?" I ask as we pass the mall. It's too late to do anything tonight, but I will make time for him in the next few days if need be.

"It'd be nice to pick up a few things, but I don't really need to do it before classes start," he responds, never looking up from his papers. "I need some shirts because mine are getting tight in the arms."

"Oh, I don't know about that. I'm personally a fan of the way your t-shirts seem about ready to rip at the seams," I say huskily. "Besides, it's proof of how hard you've been working this summer."

"God, Chad's right! You are turning into a dirty old man!" Austin closes the folder on the lap and slides it beside the seat right before I reach over to slap his leg.

"What's up with everyone suddenly making a big deal about my age? I'm not *that old*. If this keeps up, I may develop a complex." I'm kidding, but this is twice in one night someone has acted as though I'm walking up the front steps to the nursing home.

Austin smirks at me and is suddenly very interested in everything outside the car. I poke him in the side, which garners a squeal, but gets me no closer to him revealing whatever secret he's keeping.

I can think of a dozen things I would like to be doing the first weekend after the start of a school year, none of which include driving over three hours to be in the Northwoods by eleven in the morning. Unfortunately, my best friend and my boyfriend have been conspiring to get me up here and I am powerless to resist their combined charm. If I'm honest, I am looking forward to a relaxing weekend celebrating both Labor

Day and my thirty-sixth birthday. According to Austin, this should be a more traumatic milestone than my thirtieth because it marks the day I am officially closer to both forty than thirty and fifty than twenty. I never thought about age very much, but that factoid combined with the never-ending jokes about my age have me feeling as if I already have one foot in the grave.

"Austin, is there something you forgot to tell me?" I ask, taking in the sight of four cars in the driveway rather than the one I was expecting.

"Hmmm?" Austin mumbles, still curled up in the seat next to me. It's nice to see that one of us will be well rested today. He didn't even make it to the Interstate before he was sound asleep.

"Who all is going to be here this weekend?" If Chad invited some of the guys from the office or some of his other friends, that's cool, but it would have been nice to know what to expect because once I wrapped my mind around the fact that I couldn't get out of coming up here, I started looking forward to endless hours on the lake.

"Oh, are we here?" Austin scrubs at his eyes struggling to wake up. I love watching him when he is in this limbo between awake and asleep. "Chad and I thought it would be nice to make this more than just another weekend at the cabin. He suggested that I invite my mom, Amanda, and Tyler so we can spend time with them without having to worry about drama."

"That sounds great." It really does, too. The only thing that could make it better would be if—"Holy crap! How did you manage to get her up here?"

Standing on the front steps, my own mother's face looks ready to crack with the width of her smile. I quickly park the car and rush over to her, sweeping her off the ground in my arms. "David Allen, put me down before you break something," she scolds. Over her head, I can see everyone peeking through the bay window overlooking the deck.

"I can't believe you're here! How did you—when did you--" I like to think of myself as above average intelligence and possessing an impressive vocabulary, but seeing my mother after two years apart renders me speechless. I am content to simply look at her, taking in the subtle changes that come with age. Overall, she's looking better than I have ever seen her. Older, yes, but there's a light I don't remember seeing in her before. "You look great, Mom!"

"Oh, baloney. I'm saggy and wrinkled and gray. But you're a wonderful son for lying to me." She kisses both of my cheeks and then instantly forgets that I exist as Austin reaches the top step. "David, who is this devastatingly handsome man?"

"Mom, this is my boyfriend, Austin. Austin, this is my mother, Judy." My heart swells as I watch her give him the same affectionate greeting I received.

"Mrs. Becker, it's a pleasure to meet you," Austin says politely. I hide my amusement behind a fake cough because I know how well my mother handles formalities. When she speaks, I mouth the words along with her.

"Son, I am far too young to be referred to as Mrs. You can call me Barb or Mom, but nothing else," she scolds playfully. It's not until Sarah and Amanda step outside that Mom lets go of Austin. Had she continued much longer, I would have been tempted to remind her that he's both gay and unavailable, but I'm unsure which of them that would have embarrassed more.

"Sarah, you look well. Thank you for coming down

for the weekend," I greet Austin's mom warmly. She actually looks amazing. Healthy. Happy. But I keep that list of adjectives to myself because I don't want to bring up anything unpleasant this weekend.

"Thank you, David. Austin asked me to meet your mother at the airport, and I thought it would be a brilliant idea. I knew she had to be a great person to have raised such a wonderful son," Austin's mom gushes.

Within the hour, I have let go of my annoyance because I'm surrounded by every person who truly matters in my life.

Chapter Seventeen

Austin

By the third week of school, David and I have settled into a routine that works for us. He drops me off down the block from my first class before heading to his office, and I spend my afternoons in the Union or hanging out with Bree until David's done for the day.

It's abundantly clear that Casey has written me off. Even when I see him sitting at the park with his girlfriend, he's gone by the time I reach them. Bree tries covering for him, but she's a shitty liar. I haven't bothered to ask whether it's my orientation or the fact that I took the lifeline I was offered because it really doesn't matter. I made a promise to myself that I wouldn't dwell on fickle people, so it's up to him to talk to me or not.

That doesn't mean he's not on my mind every day. If he would talk to me, I would thank him because he's a big part of the reason I know what I want to do with my life now. I still have to figure out what degree is going to be most beneficial, but between my own circumstances and his, I want to work with young adults on the streets. I want to be the one to teach them that life can get better, but the only way it will is if they're willing to put in the hard work.

When my second class of the day starts, I'm so engrossed in last minute studying for the next class that I barely hear the door open and close at the front of the lecture hall. If I had, I wouldn't have jumped when I heard a familiar voice echoing off the ceiling.

David

Who can tell me what creates an ideal society?" I ask as soon as the alarm on my phone chimes, alerting me that it is ten o'clock. I take one last sip of my coffee, setting it on the stool behind the podium. I should have said I couldn't take over this class for the next two weeks, but there was no graceful way to bow out when the department head approached me. I sent Austin a text message warning him, but from the stunned look on his ghost-white face when I turn around, he had already turned off his phone for the day.

Silence fills the room while every student tries to come up with what they think is the right answer. Most of the time, I would be amused by their reluctance to give a wrong answer, but today I just want someone to say something. Until I have a chance to email Marcus Dombrowski and get a feel for his plans for the time he will be missing due to a family emergency, I have to get these kids thinking.

"Come on, people," I urge impatiently. I click the button on the remote to dim the lights as the first slide in the PowerPoint presentation I found on Marcus's desk appears on the screen behind me. "This isn't rocket science. We're here to discuss and learn about societies. That's something every one of you should be familiar with, unless you're so engrossed in your phones that you don't realize there's a world around you. Now, someone tell me one thing that would help form a perfect society in your own mind."

"Equality." The answer, which is usually one of the first five thrown out every time I ask this question, comes from a young woman in the second row. Her choice is vague and idealistic, but it's a start.

"Good." I look down at the seating chart to find the girl's name. "Thank you Miss Andrews. Let's discuss what equality means in an ideal society."

I write the term in large red letters on the white board, underlining it for effect. When I turn my attention back to the room, I begin to wonder if some of the students opted to take this class because it would allow them a mid-morning nap. Their eyes are vacant and a few can't even be bothered to pretend they're paying attention.

Glancing at the chart again, I decide to make an example of one of the slackers in the back row. My patience and understanding does not extend to those who choose to waste my time and theirs. "Mister Thompson, what does equality mean to you?"

The student practically jumps out of his seat at my stern tone. He looks to the student next to him and she shrugs. The two of them will make an amazing team someday. "Uh, I guess it means...you know... treating everyone the same, even if they're different." A few girls giggle while his friends roll their eyes at his elementary answer.

"Okay, but can you give me some examples of inequality in our own society that would need to be corrected if we were trying to form an ideal society?" I urge, hoping beyond hope that this kid simply isn't firing on all cylinders this morning.

"Not really, man. I mean, back in the sixties there was a lot of change to be made, but I think we've come a long way since then. I think everyone's pretty much treated the same now."

"Bullshit!" The outburst comes from the other end of the back row. I turn to the white board quickly to hide the twisted expression on my face. I pinch the bridge of my nose, trying to figure out how to best proceed. No one in this room knows that I know Austin outside of a professional capacity and I would prefer to keep it that way. Unfortunately, I already know where this argument is headed and it's one that the entire class needs to hear.

I glance at the seating chart, just as I have every time I have called on a student so far. Austin doesn't seem worried right now; his expression is filled with pent-up rage.

"Mister Pritchard, would you care to elaborate?" I ask, cocking my head when I see the other student slump back in his chair. "While I wouldn't have chosen to voice my opinion the way you did, I have to agree with your statement. Now, I would be interested to hear why you feel Mister Thompson's logic is faulty."

Austin worries his lip between his teeth while he picks at the faded screen-printing on his t-shirt. When he looks back to the front of the room, a bit of confidence returns to his gaze.

"Because our society sucks at treating people equally," he argues. He leans forward in his chair, once again staring down his fellow student. "You'd have to be blind to think there's anything close to equality in the world we live in. At best, there is equality within social circles, but that doesn't mean shit when we look down on those who don't make as much money as we do or don't follow the same belief systems we hold.

"Every single person in this room can likely recite the groups of people who are protected by anti-discrimination acts, but even that's a farce." Austin becomes more animated the longer he speaks. I lean against the table behind me, allowing him to essentially present one of the lessons that typically follows this particular discussion.

"That's an interesting point of view, Mister Pritchard," I praise him.

"Austin. Please don't call me Mister Pritchard. He and I are nothing alike." I bite my tongue to keep from telling him that I am well aware how different the two of them are. I knew it would upset him, but I couldn't very well address him by first name when I have used a more formal greeting for anyone else. I make a mental note to tell him tonight just how proud I am of the way he has come into his own recently.

"Duly noted," I respond, nodding for him to continue.

"We all live in our own little bubbles, surrounded by people who are like us. We don't stop to think about how our actions affect others. If you walk five blocks from here, you'll see pockets of homeless people. In an ideal society, you would stop to help them, or even to just say hello, but I'd be willing to bet most people in this room would walk by as if they didn't notice those in need. You probably already have, but because they aren't directly threatening you, you don't even see them."

His rant continues for the next eight captivating minutes. Every body in the room is turned to face him, most genuinely interested in his views. When he finishes, we all sit in stunned silence. This time, I'm certain the vacant expressions on my students' faces are caused by the realization that their classmate has opened their eyes to a critical flaw in the makeup of our society.

Austin spends the rest of the class hunched over his notebook. He makes no further attempt to participate in the conversation regarding the differences between an equality-based society and one created out of different social classes.

Before I can call out to Austin to see me once the room clears, he's out the door. That doesn't please me, but it is for the best that we have some space right now because emotions are running high and I don't trust myself to maintain an appropriate distance. Oh, who am I kidding? I want to thread my fingers through his hair and hold his face to mine, kissing him until he's gasping for breath.

At the end of the day, I wait for Austin outside the Union. It's the first time we've met on campus, but he had a study group that ran long so he didn't have time to walk to our normal meeting spot, and I have zero patience to wait for him after that little display in class this morning. I have repeatedly told Austin that it isn't an issue that we are in a relationship, but today I'm the one whose heart is racing at the thought of someone seeing us together. Life was cut and dry just a few short weeks ago; we had done everything possible to ensure there could be no accusations that I am fraternizing with a student. I have no problem explaining that to anyone who might ask, but it is a hassle I'm not looking forward to.

"What are you doing here?" Austin asks as he casually strolls across the parking lot. "I thought we were going to meet down at the ramp."

I take his hand in mine, leading him to the passenger side of the car. "Sue me, I didn't want to wait long enough for you to walk down there." Leaning in, I gently kiss his cheek.

To his credit, Austin presses his body into mine, hugging me tightly. It's not until we're both settled into the car that I see how nervous he is. He's chewing on the corner of his thumb, watching me out of the corner of his eye, waiting for me to scold him for his rant in class today. I lace my fingers through his to spare the skin from being gnawed to the bone. "What's going on?" I ask him, leaving it up to him to broach the subject.

"Am I going to need to change my schedule again?" he asks in response. "I s'pose that's a stupid question. Of course I'm going to have to drop. It's not like you can just stop teaching." Austin beats his hand against the inside of the car door, angry that he's the one who has to make a change. But he doesn't. As far as I'm concerned, this is a temporary situation and there's no reason to derail his goals.

"I think that is a perfectly valid question. Your courses are important to you, so it makes sense that that is your primary concern, but no, you won't have to drop the class." Austin settles back in his seat, no longer abusing my upholstery. "I should only be filling in for Professor Dombrowski for two weeks while he handles a personal matter. At that point, he will take over the teaching of his class and I will regain my office time."

"What about assignments and exams? As soon as you even look at one of my papers the wrong way, someone's going to bitch."

"First, as long as we aren't flaunting our relationship in the lecture hall, I don't think that will be a problem. And second, there are no exams scheduled in that time. There will be a project, but it won't be due before everything is back to normal."

By the time I pull into the parking lot of the restaurant where I had planned to take Austin for dinner, he's sound asleep in the passenger seat. He's been holding up better than I expected, but between the insane number of classes he is taking and the mountains of billing Chad seems to have neglected for the past six months, Austin hasn't gotten to bed before two in the morning for the past week. Rather than wake him, I leave the car running and head inside to pick up a to-go order. By taking it home, we will also be able to speak more freely about his concerns.

Austin

I really don't need more shit stressing me out, but every time I walk through the doors of the social sciences building, I can't help but wonder if today is the day someone finds out that I'm fucking one of my professors. When that happens, it won't matter that we've been in a relationship for a while now, no one will believe that I'm not doing this in an effort to get an easy A. David keeps telling me I'm being paranoid, but this could fuck both of us. While I'm sure I would be able to get past it, he's putting his career on the line every time we walk through the front door and spend the night together.

"What's your deal, Pritchard?" Rob Thompson flicks the papers on my desk as he shoves past me. Rumor has it he wasn't too happy about me calling him on his shit two weeks ago and he's made it his mission to make my life miserable. Luckily, I only have to see him twice a week.

"Excuse me?" I respond, not bothering to look up from the stack of articles I printed out last night for my first psych paper of the semester.

"Ever since that new prof came in, you've turned into the teacher's pet." Every inch of my body from my head to my asshole clenches at his accusation. I struggle to steady my breath so I won't give away the secret I've been carrying around. For all I know, this jackass is just pissed that I *love* showing the world what an ignorant prick he is. "Even worse is the way he lets you run off at the mouth with whatever tangent you decide to grab. Makes me wonder if there's something going on between the two of you."

I've always thought people were kidding when they said the world starts to disappear around them when they reach their breaking point, but as everything in my periphery goes dark, I see what they're talking about. The conversations that were crystal clear moments ago become muted as my senses shut down. I can't fucking breathe and my stomach is churning. I'm vaguely aware of my head hitting the desk as a panic attack settles in.

"Whoa, calm the fuck down," Rob says, crouching in front of me. "You're seriously fucked in the head, kid." When I lift my head the few inches I'm capable of, I see genuine concern in his eyes. He's still an idiot, but maybe he's not quite as much of a prick as I originally thought.

"You're one to talk," I spit back. My mind is racing, trying to think of a plausible excuse for my reaction, other than admitting that I am indeed fucking one of my professors and love how well he knows my body. "Sorry, not feeling too hot this morning."

I start shoving papers into my bag, not giving a shit if everything winds up crumpled at the bottom of the backpack. I have to get the fuck out of here before I totally lose my shit.

"I feel ya," Rob responds sympathetically. "I learned my lesson last year, so now I save the hard partying for the weekends. You'd probably be smart to do the same."

"Thanks for the tip," I call out over my shoulder as I leave the room. That proves to be a mistake because I see David at the front of the class cautiously watching me. I pull my phone out of the pocket of my hoodie and shoot him a quick text letting him know I'm going to crash at Bree's until he's done, because I'm not feeling well. Might as well ride out this lie as far as I need.

Chapter Eighteen

Austin

After sprinting through Library Mall and the first two blocks of State Street, I double over to catch my breath. And possibly to puke my guts out. "Austin!" I turn around and see Bree jogging up the sidewalk, weaving her way through midday shoppers. "What's going on? You're white as a damn sheet."

"Someone knows," I mutter, leaning against the wall because my legs are about ready to buckle under me. "Can we go to your place?"

"Yeah, of course!" She takes me by the hand, leading me through the narrow alley behind the buildings so I don't have to deal with people. Casey's a fucking idiot if he lets her go because of his hang-ups. She motions for me to lead the way up the dark stairwell, which may not be a great idea because I'm still not terribly steady on my feet. "You get settled on the couch and I'm going to make some tea while I make a phone call. Ten minutes later and I wouldn't have seen you. I'm supposed to meet up with a couple of classmates today, but they'll understand."

"Bree, you don't have to do that," I say, my voice whiny and unsteady. "If you don't mind me hanging out here until David's done, I'll be fine. I just...I couldn't be at the school right now."

"Yeah, about that, you need to start from the top and tell me why you're all fucked up." She's got that 'don't fuck with me' tone in her voice and I do exactly as she demanded and tell her all about how David was asked to take over my class for a few weeks while the instructor was out for whatever reason, and how David couldn't figure out how to get out of it without admitting that we're together.

Sometimes, I feel like his dirty little secret, but then I remember that this is temporary and not in every part of his life. There's a legitimate reason no one at the university can know about the two of us, but now I'm seeing how foolish it was to think we could keep the world from knowing.

"This was supposed to be the last day he's in there, but his department head called last week to let him know it was going to be at least one more week." I sip the steaming tea, curling my lip at the heavy ginger flavor. It might be good for my stomach, but it tastes like shit. "And then this morning this guy started talking shit about me and said he thinks I'm fucking David and that's why he lets me ramble, as he put it."

"Are you sure he knows anything?" Bree asks, curling her legs beneath her on the cushion next to me. "It seems to me like he's one of those arrogant assholes who think they're better than everyone. I'd bet he was doing exactly what you said: talking shit."

"Really? So, of all the insults he could have come

up with, he just happened to pull out the one that's the truth? I don't think so." I shake my head to prove my point. My phone buzzes and I debate whether or not to answer it. I decide to ignore it for the time being because I'm not in the mood to deal with anyone. I just want to pull the curtains and sit here in the dark, wallowing in self-pity.

Bree begins lightly rubbing my back when the darkness starts creeping in again threatening to pull me under. I'm beginning to wonder if I should take the frequency of my panic attacks as a sign that I'm fucking up my life, because they rarely happened before I met David. Come to think of it, I *never* had them until I came out.

"Okay, I still think you're freaking about nothing, but let's say he's right. David's only going to be teaching that class for another week, right?" I nod, cradling the ceramic mug in my hands. "Then I don't see the problem. He's not technically the professor."

"I guess you're right, but this could seriously fuck him over if anyone finds out. We talked about it when I was registering for classes and he was very clear that he couldn't be in a position of authority over me, otherwise he'd be reprimanded and possibly lose his job." My phone goes off again and I reach into my pocket to turn it off. I'll look at the missed calls soon, but not just yet.

"Then it sounds like you need to drop the class, just to be on the safe side." She leans forward to grab her laptop, pulling up the university's information on adding and dropping classes. "Hmm, it looks like you're going to have a tough time there as well. If you drop, you'll only get half your tuition credited and that shit can't be cheap over there."

"That won't fucking work," I groan, imagining holding a lighter to six one-hundred dollar bills because it's about the same thing. If I drop, I'm going to be losing over a week's pay and that's not acceptable. "Can I switch classes?"

I lean over to look at the screen with her. This is why I love Bree; since day one, she's had a way of pulling me back from the edge when I flip out. "Well, it looks like you can still technically add a class, but only with the approval of the department head. You could call to see if you can make an even switch, basically just changing the time you're attending that course, but I'm not sure what the policy is on that."

"Fuck, I'm basically screwed." I slam the mug down on the coffee table a bit harder than intended. "If I go to the department head, I'm going to have to tell him *why* I want to switch, and I can't do that. I won't lie to him, but I also can't tell him that David and I have been a couple since summer because that would sound fishy."

"So find a way to spin it in your favor. Don't tell him that you're fucking like bunnies, but let him know that there's a conflict of interest," she suggests. "Or you could just sit back and chill the fuck out like I already told you to do."

"Yeah, you're probably right."

"Honey, I *know* I'm right." She laughs, pulling an afghan off the back of the couch and kissing my temple as she gets up. "Now, you get some rest and I'm going to work on a painting I have to turn in next week."

"Aren't you supposed to meet your friends?" I feel bad for screwing up today for both of us. I fully intend to take her advice and get some sleep, so there's no point in her sitting here watching me.

"Yeah, but they're all rich little bitches with their fancy cameras they'll never use," she says, scrunching her face in disgust. "I'd much rather chill here with you. I just have to make sure I head down to tell Casey what's going on in a few hours. What time is the sexy professor done today?"

"Five, I think. He's been staying later to make up for the lost office time." I close my eyes and drift off to sleep before she responds.

David

"D o you have a minute?" John Parks, the head of the sociology department, asks just as I finish putting papers into my messenger bag to take home with me. I debated canceling my office hours this afternoon so I could find out what happened this morning, but there were two students who had verified their appointments with me before class and I didn't feel right postponing my time with them for what's probably nothing more than a stomach bug. Still, I hate that I haven't seen or heard from Austin since he raced out of the lecture hall this morning.

"Yes, what can I do for you?" I motion for him to take a seat and wait until he's settled before sitting down. Beneath my desk, I'm wringing my hands, concerned that he has come to find me. Typically, when John wants to talk, he prefers to use email or the phone.

"I have some bad news," he begins, his face unreadable and his voice stern. "Marcus called me this morning to let me know he will be filing paperwork for FMLA. Apparently, his mother isn't doing well and he needs to stay with her a while longer. I suggested he use this time for his mandatory sabbatical and he's agreed. I know it's far from ideal for the department, but I would rather he be able to focus his attention on his family the way I would any other member of our department."

"I'm sorry to hear that, sir. And I think we all appreciate your concern for our personal lives as well as the professional." Bile inches up my throat, knowing that there are limits to this man's generosity.

"Yes, well that's why I'm here today. I know you already have a full plate, but I was hoping you could continue leading the sessions you took on temporarily. I have started looking for a replacement, but we all know that takes time and I'm not certain it will happen this semester."

I feel as though I'm racing toward a brick wall with no way to stop. This poses a huge problem because Austin cannot stay in the class if I'm the official professor, but I can't refuse this request because it's not really a request at all. I'm the new guy here, which means, I am the one who will be dumped on when things like this happen. Fair or not, it is the way every school I have taught at works.

"Of course, sir." The moment I agree, John stands and I take his proffered hand. Now, I have to figure out the best way to bring this up to Austin while he is already feeling under the weather.

"Good, we will be sending notification to all students by midday tomorrow so they will be aware of the change. Have a good night, David." I mumble a response because my mind has already left the building. Realistically, I have about twelve hours at most to sit down with Austin to find a solution.

Austin looks awful when he opens the door to Bree's apartment. It is a testament to how he's feeling that he even gave me her address. Up until now, this place has been his little sanctuary and I haven't pushed him to share it with me.

"Hey, are you okay?" I ask, tucking a lock of hair behind his ear as I kiss his cheek.

"Yeah, just a stomach bug. I'm going to crash here tonight so I don't get you sick." Even if that was an acceptable suggestion, the fact that he won't look at me tells me he's lying. I thought we were past the major bumps, but tonight it seems as if we are both holding something back from the other. The part of me that remembers how skittish he has been in the past wants to take the easy way out and tell him that it's fine, but I can't do that. I can't risk him finding out what I was just told by email rather than hear it from me.

"Austin, if you aren't feeling well, you need to be home in your own bed. In *our* bed," I say sternly. I push the door closed and reach for his backpack, throwing it over my shoulder. He stares at me for a moment, likely debating whether or not to fight me before his shoulders slump and he shuffles across the room for his shoes.

"Hey, David!" Bree calls out from the back of the small apartment. I didn't even realize she was here. "Austin, remember what I told you. Now, get your ass out of here so I can go spend some time with my man."

The words are right, but the agitated tone of Bree's voice tells me she may not be as anxious as she's trying to appear. Austin hasn't shared much with me, but I do know Bree and her situation with Casey was a big part of why Austin quit fighting with me about not paying half of all the bills.

"Ready?" I ask when he stands. He nods and then

walks back to say goodbye to Bree. The way he is acting, I wonder if the email has already gone out to the students. I follow him down the stairs like a prisoner to the guillotine. Tonight is going to be a long night.

I don't pressure Austin to tell me what's really going through his mind while we are driving home. I want to give him my undivided attention, and I'm honestly not sure I can trust him right this minute to not run away at the first stop light. Him suggesting that he could stay at Bree's tonight rather than coming home has me on edge.

When we get to the house, Austin heads directly for the office. His backpack is still in the car, so I know he's not working on anything for school. While I appreciate his dedication to working for Chad, I'm not going to let him continue avoiding me.

"Austin, can I talk to you for a moment?" I ask after rapping my knuckles on the office door. Without waiting for an invitation, I settle into one of the club chairs in front of the window. "I had a visit from Dr. Parks this afternoon. It seems Professor Dombrowski is going to be out the rest of the semester."

"Fuck," Austin groans, bending at the waist to rest his head on the desk. "Today just keeps getting better and better."

"I take it you didn't know?" I thought for certain that was what had him tied in knots, but figured it would be better for me to share rather than ask if he knew because Austin is in one of his moods where he's holding everything in.

"No, but that's just fucking great." I walk behind him and begin massaging his shoulders. Yes, this is a setback, but he's taking the news far harder than I expected.

"After weighing the options you have, there are two

viable solutions. The first is that you drop the course and I will put the fifty-percent you're going to lose into a savings account for next semester." He stiffens at the suggestion, just as I knew he would. Austin would rather suffer than ask me for a dime, so I know this isn't acceptable to him but I put it out there anyway. "Second, you stay in the class and we will be extra careful."

"No way! I can't stay there if you're officially taking on the class." The casters on the chair ram into my bare feet and I stifle the scream that wants to come out. Austin pushes himself up and begins pacing around the room.

"Austin, hear me out here," I plead. "You and I both know I won't go easier on you than any other student in my class. If anything, I will be tougher on you because I know what you are capable of. Therefore, if we are diligent, making sure no one finds out, there is no issue."

"David, I love you and I love that you're trying to fix this, but I can't let you do that." Austin's going to wear a hole in the carpet and wind up bald with as much as he's fretting right now. I place my hands on his arms, holding tight to keep him from going anywhere. "Besides, it's too late. Rob made a comment to me this morning about you giving me preferential treatment because we're fucking. Don't you get it? Our secret's out and there's nothing either of us can do about it. Now, it's just a matter of time before Dr. Parks finds out, and when that happens, you'll be out of a job and I'll probably have an F on my official transcript."

I feel as if the air has been knocked out of my lungs and I can't draw a breath. I am certain my boss has no clue what is going on as of yet, because he would have mentioned it to me if he did. "Austin, I spent almost thirty minutes talking to Dr. Parks today and he mentioned nothing of the sort. Unless you have said something to someone, I don't know how Mr. Thompson would have found out about us."

"You seriously think I would have said something?" Austin screeches. He jerks out of my grasp and walks over to the windows, staring out at the rainy night. "For fuck's sake, David! I thought you knew me better than that. I am well aware of what's on the line for you if anyone knows, so I've tried to go out of my way to not even look at you unless absolutely necessary. No, I haven't told anyone, but thanks for the vote of confidence."

Austin storms out of the room, slamming the door behind him. I close my eyes and take a few breaths before following him, hoping to calm myself so I don't say anything I will regret in the morning.

I open the door to our bedroom, only to find the lights off and the room untouched. Across the hall, muffled sobs seep under the door of the guest bedroom. I open the door, closing it all but a crack as I make my way to Austin. There is a certain security to be had in the dark, a shot of courage in the knowledge that we can both speak without having to see one another.

"Austin, I never said I thought you said something," I whisper as I sit on the edge of the bed next to him. "Your revelation took me by surprise, much as his words did you this morning. I was simply thinking out loud and shouldn't have."

"I don't know if I can keep doing this, David," Austin cries. "I'm not sure how I'm going to walk away, but I know that everything you have here is what you've dreamed of. I won't be the one to make you lose that."

I lie down next to Austin, curling my body around

his. I tease the skin on his stomach as I kiss the shell of his ear, hoping he will settle to sleep and we can talk about this once our nerves aren't so frayed. Before long, soft snores fill the room and I pry myself away from him, giving Austin the space he wants. For now. "Someday, you will understand that *you* are part of the everything I have here," I whisper against his neck. "Without you, the rest of it means nothing to me. I love you, Austin. We'll talk about this tomorrow."

"I love you, too," he mumbles, squeezing my hand for a moment before rolling onto his stomach. I make my way across the hall, closing his bedroom door and leaving mine wide open. The move is partly an invitation and partly so I will hear him if he tries to get up in the night.

Chapter Nineteen

Austin

I wake up in the morning feeling like I've been hit by a Mack truck that decided to turn around and take another pass at me for good measure. The sour stomach from yesterday is nearly unbearable; my eyes feel like sandpaper and my mouth like a cotton ball. I cautiously open my eyes after reaching out to find the other side of the bed empty and sit up too quickly, trying to figure out where I am. It slowly dawns on me that I'm in the guest room of David's house. That upsets me, until I remember that I'm the one who ran in here and slammed the door last night.

The smell of coffee brewing acts as a beacon and I stumble toward it, needing a healthy dose of caffeine and a huge glass of water. "Good morning," David greets me. He sounds almost as depressed as I'm feeling today, but I don't know how to fix it for either of us.

Well, that's not totally true. I know what I need to do about the academic situation, but there's no guarantee that will do shit about what's going on here. I was a petulant little brat last night and I wouldn't blame David if he says I've hit some sort of limit. I step behind him, wrapping my arms around his waist with my head resting on his chest while he makes breakfast. "I'm sorry I was such an asshole to you last night."

"You weren't," he lies. He turns in my arms so we're chest to chest. "Okay, so you were, but I understand why. I don't know what the answer is, but we will find it. I think right now both of us have to have faith in the other that it will work out however it is meant to."

"I know, and you're right," I agree. I'm not telling him what I'm going to do just yet because I need to spend my free time this morning brainstorming the best approach. "Yesterday was a super shitty day. I'm glad it's behind us."

We sit together in the breakfast nook, him reading the paper while I surf the internet on my phone. He is one of the few people I know who still read an honest-to-god newspaper every day. I'd much rather pull up the paper's website and get the highlights without all the other crap.

After we're done eating, we finish our morning routines the same way we have every other day since school started. He goes upstairs to get ready for school while I clean up the breakfast dishes and run the dishwasher before pulling on the first clothes my hands land on.

We chat on the drive downtown, both of us cautiously avoiding the subject of the class that can no longer be. He gives me a kiss when he parks at the very top of the parking ramp and reminds me that we're going to Chad's for dinner tonight. It's become a weekly activity I love. Next to Bree, Becky is one of my best friends and we have fun pointing out the hot guys on TV while Chad and David do much manlier things. It's a balance that works for all of us.

The closer the clock creeps to eleven, the more nervous I become. I'm holding onto the slightest sliver of hope that I will be able to slide into a different class without any penalties, but even that requires department head approval.

"Austin, Dr. Parks will see you now," his secretary says sweetly. It's that condescending voice that I think is a required skill for anyone in her position.

"It's good to see you, Austin. Please, have a seat." I have only met this man once, and yet he makes it seem as if this is a regular occurrence. I sit at the edge of the chair, not wanting to appear too comfortable in his space. "What can I help you with today?"

I clear my throat, running over each possible angle for this conversation before I begin. "Sir, I need to transfer out of my sociological theory course. I have looked through the course catalog and found a different time that I feel will be a better fit for me."

It's not better, not by a long shot, but this is my attempt at being as vague as possible. I will have to run from one block to the next between classes, but it's doable.

"Austin, we are already six weeks into class. I'm not certain it would be wise for you to add a new class so far into the term," he advises, steepling his hands in front of his face. "Does this have anything to do with the email that was sent this morning regarding Professor Becker?"

Shit. What am I supposed to say to that? I promised myself I wasn't going to lie, but now he's asked me flat-out if it's because of him. I panic. "Yes, sir," I respond quickly, instantly hating myself. "I mean, not exactly, sir."

"Well, which is it?" Dr. Parks leans forward in his leather chair and I shrink back in my seat. I wring the back of my neck, suddenly feeling the heat in his office. "Austin, if you have an issue with a member of the faculty, you need to be comfortable voicing those concerns. Now, if there is something barring you from feeling that you will be able to learn from Professor Becker, I need to know."

"What?" I ask, swallowing hard, hoping my voice returns to the proper octave soon. "No, it's nothing like that! Professor Becker is a great instructor, but as I said, I need to be allowed to switch to the other session because of my schedule."

Shit. Shit. Shit. The look on Dr. Parks's face tells me I've just fucked up. This is why I wasn't going to lie to him; I can't lie for shit. "Austin, if you can't be honest with me regarding the reason you are trying to change classes six weeks into the semester, I don't see how I can help you. Would you like a moment to consider your answer before I ask you again? Be warned, I will *only* ask you one more time."

"No sir, that won't be necessary." I know I should look at him, show him the respect someone in his position is due, but I'm too ashamed of how poorly I'm handling this situation. "I'm sorry I wasn't more open with you from the beginning, but David and I know one another outside of the classroom, through mutual friends. Because of that, I'm hoping to minimize any opportunity for anyone to claim favoritism if that becomes public knowledge."

"I see," he responds, sitting back in a more relaxed position as he stares at me over the top of his glasses.

"And have you talked to David about this? I appreciate what you are trying to do, but that doesn't change the fact that this is a highly unusual request."

"I haven't talked to him, sir. I understand that you don't make a habit of approving changes, but you need to know I chose this session specifically because I didn't want either of us in this position. Now, I feel my only options are to either shift my schedule or drop the class." And lose the money. Damn, I don't want that to happen.

Dr. Parks sits quietly, tapping away at something on his keyboard. I fidget, worried that I've just made things even worse than they were yesterday, pressing my lips together to keep from begging him to say something. The longer he doesn't acknowledge me or give me any indication of what he's thinking, the more nervous I become.

"It seems to me you have quite the predicament," Dr. Parks states bluntly. "You're not incorrect in saying it's highly unusual that I will grant a transfer request once the classes are established and the cut-off date has passed. With your situation, I feel as if my hands are tied, which is a feeling I do not enjoy. I will need to look into this further and get back to you. You can expect to hear from me within the week one way or the other. Until then, I would suggest you avoid seeing David outside of the lecture hall in order to minimize the chance of anyone filing a complaint and forcing me to take administrative action."

"Yes, sir," I respond quietly. I swallow hard around the lump in my throat, wondering how in the hell I'm supposed to not see David, but unwilling to argue with the man in front of me. To say anything would only dig the hole deeper.

"If there's nothing else..." Dr. Parks effectively dismisses me, turning his attention to a legal pad in front of him. I stand and thank him for his time on my way out the door.

I barely remember walking out of the building or across the library mall on my way to find Bree and Casey. She doesn't have classes today, so it's unlikely I will be able to spend time with one and not the other unless Casey's doing day labor again today. The two of them are sitting close on one of the concrete steps having a heated discussion, but the moment they see me, Casey takes off yet again. I can't believe I once thought he was a real friend because the way he's acted lately makes me feel like he'd rather step in a pile of shit than talk to me.

"Hey, what the fuck's up his ass this time?" I ask, sitting down next to Bree.

When she looks up at me, her eyes are swollen and red, the last of her tears still evident in wet trails down her face. "I told him I can't do this anymore," she sighs. "I tried, Austin, you know I did. But I'm sick of not really sleeping at night because I'm freaked out that someone's going to steal Casey's shit or fuck with us. I'm having problems staying awake in my classes. It's just all too much. I really thought that if I explained it to him, he'd get it and agree to stay with me..."

She offers a weak smile to a girl with a magenta fauxhawk when she says hello. I drape my arm over her shoulders, figuring that a hug is about the only comfort I can give her right about now. "I take it that didn't happen?"

"No," she sobs. "He tried turning it around on me, saying I don't understand how hard life is for him. God, he was such an asshole that I can't help but wonder if this is just a game to him. I mean, look at you; you had nowhere to go and swallowed your pride when someone who loved you offered to help you out. That's all I was trying to do for him."

If she said something like that to Casey, I suppose I can't blame the guy for looking like he wanted to punch me in the face. No man wants to hear that he's a fuck up and too stupid to do what another man does, even when it's true. No, it wasn't easy for me to accept David's help, but I did and I don't regret it.

My phone chimes and I see that I have a text message from the same man who consumes so many of my thoughts.

Dr. Parks wants to meet with me at four. Can you go to Bree's for a while?

I type and delete my response several times before hitting the call button. I have to tell him what I did because there's no fucking way this is a coincidence. Dr. Parks didn't seem pissed off when I left, but he definitely wasn't happy to hear what I had to say today.

"Hey, you didn't have to call me right away," David says as soon as he answers the phone. "I know it's not typically an issue, but I wanted you to know that I'm going to be delayed."

"Yeah, about that..." I close my eyes and count to ten before continuing because I *really* don't want to fess up to being an idiot. One of these times, David's going to believe me and then Casey and I can keep one another company through the winter. "I have something to tell you and you're probably going to be pissed at me."

"Austin, what's going on?" Concern laces David's rich voice, making it even harder to find my words.

"I talked to Dr. Parks this morning about transferring to a different session of the class," I admit, not stopping to take a breath as I explain the logic behind my visit. "I tried telling him it was because of a schedule conflict, but when it became obvious that wasn't going to be enough to get him to make the change, I told him that we know one another on a personal level."

"You WHAT?" David shrieks. No matter what stupid shit I've done since we met, I don't think I've ever heard him raise his voice to me. I cradle the phone between my ear and shoulder, doubling over to take deep breaths before I have a full-blown panic attack.

"I'm sorry, David," I apologize. "There's no way I can stay in your class, I won't even take the chance of someone filing a complaint and you getting in trouble. This was the only solution, other than dropping the class."

"And you didn't think that you should talk to me about this? This is *my job*, Austin. If I lose it, I will be forced to sell my house and find a job with another university, if they'll have me," he growls. I want to point out that that is *exactly* what I was trying to avoid, but he's not letting me get a single word in. "How many times have I told you that you have to talk to me? Now, thanks to you not bothering to think about the consequences and see if there was any other way, you have proven to me that you are lying to me every time you tell me you trust me."

"I'm not, David," I cry. Bree and I must make quite the sight because now she's the one comforting me while I'm sobbing like a fucking baby. "I *do* trust you, but I also have to be a man sometimes and do what's best for me without expecting you to clean up my messes."

"Oh, I don't think you have to worry about that this time," he says sarcastically. "I have to go sit down with Dr. Parks in a little bit and there will be plenty of your mess for me to clean up. I have to go, I'll talk to you later."

The line goes dead and I stare at the phone, willing him to call back. "Fuck!" I wind up to throw my phone but think better of it.

"Come on, Austin," Bree says, offering me a hand to help me off the pitted concrete. "Let's go curl up on my couch and compare shitty man stories."

"He's not shitty, Bree. As always, I'm the one who fucked up this time." I'd love nothing more than to make David the villain, but it's all me. I'm the one who created this mess.

"Honey, you have a penis, so I have no doubt you fucked up, but I doubt he's blameless." She laughs. We link arms and start walking up the hill to her apartment as I tell her how I managed to make a bad situation worse.

By the time we get to her place, I'm freaking the fuck out because David has never given me the silent treatment. He's actually made it abundantly clear that it's one of his pet peeves. *If you have a problem, you can't hide from it, you have to face it head-on.* His words lose some of their meaning now that he's taken a page out of my book on conflict resolution.

Chapter Twenty

David

I'm fuming by the time I walk down the hall to Dr. Parks' office. I've gotten used to Austin not always making the most mature decisions, but this time he has gone too far. He was so worried about one of his classmates being the one to disclose our relationship and then he turned around and handed Dr. Parks my career on a gilded platter. I have been trying to figure out what I can say to minimize the damage, but there is no way. I knew I was taking a chance, but foolishly thought love would overcome everything. Honestly, I may as well have had power ballads on repeat as the soundtrack of my life over the past few months.

"Please, sit." Tension is thick in the room as John stares blankly at me. He purses his lips as if he's just eaten something unpleasant. "Would you care to tell me about Austin Pritchard?"

"Sir?" It's doubtful that I am doing anything to help

my case at this point, but I decide to see what John has to say before giving him anything to hold against me.

"The boy came to me today asking for a transfer. When I pressed him to give me a compelling reason to approve such a request after the semester has been established, he informed me that the two of you know one another on a personal level."

"That is true," I confirm. I maintain eye contact out of respect for the man, but it's the hardest thing I have had to do in recent history. I want to tuck into myself like a frightened child who knows a beating is on the horizon. Perhaps I should say that we are nothing more than friends, but I refuse to stoop so low as to publicly deny Austin. No matter how upset I am over his actions and the issues they've created, I love him with my whole heart and he doesn't deserve to be hidden. I simply have to decide if I can continue the way we have been and whether or not he will ever take me at my word when I tell him the lengths I would go to in order to help him.

He crosses his arms over his chest and grins smugly as I struggle to find something to say. John chuckles at my discomfort, leaning forward. "David, being friends with a student is not against university policy. However, I am a bit concerned that this revelation was made by the student. Why didn't you mention anything when I originally asked you to take over the class, either on a temporary or permanent basis?"

"Sir, that was a poor judgment call on my part," I admit. "At first, I assumed it wouldn't be an issue because Marcus was supposed to return before any major assignments were due. And yesterday, well, my mind was elsewhere, which I understand is no excuse."

"No, it's not." He narrows his eyes, glaring at me for a moment. "I'm not sure I want to know what you were thinking because there is something to be said about plausible deniability. Now, I have to consider his request to transfer, without setting a precedent for future terms. You have to appreciate the tight spot this puts me in."

"I do, sir." I nod, cracking my knuckles one at a time to release the tiniest bit of tension from my body. "And again, I apologize for my oversight."

"Oversight," John huffs. "Yes, I suppose that is one way to put it. I won't place an official notice of reprimand in your file this time, but I have to let you know that I won't be able to overlook such lack of forethought in the future." This is the first time in my professional career that I've been reprimanded in any way and I assure John I have no plans to be in this position in the future.

We are supposed to have dinner with Chad and Becky tonight, but I am so upset I can't even talk to Austin yet. It doesn't matter that there is no administrative action; it's the fact that he doesn't trust me. He says he does, but every time his hand is forced, he turns away from me. By the time I reach my car, I have worked up a good head of steam, to the point I can't calm myself down.

I quickly dial Chad, needing a voice of reason because the more time I have to think about what Austin did, the more upset I become. "Hey, you'd better not be calling to bail on me for tonight," Chad answers.

"No, not exactly. I have a situation and I'm not sure if I have reason to be as angry as I am," I grumble.

The light turns red and my blood pressure rises a bit more. The way today is going, you would think it's a Monday.

"Wow, Mr. Smartypants is calling me for advice? This must be serious," Chad teases. I attempt to laugh, but it comes out as a pathetic croak. "What's going on that couldn't wait until you get here and have a beer or three in ya?"

I explain everything that has happened in the past two days. Chad interjects with a whistle here or a grunt there to let me know he's listening. When I finish, he's silent. I pull the phone away from my head and see that the call is still connected. "Did I lose you?"

"No, I'm here. I'm just trying to figure out what I'm supposed to say," he admits. "I would have put Becky on the phone if I knew it was this type of shit."

"I have a feeling Becky would call me an idiot, which is why I called you instead of her." I rest my head against the cool glass as I wait for the light to change. "That's the other reason I called. I'm wondering if you'd like to head out for a beer, a guys' night of sorts, the way we used to do before marriage and relationships and other complications."

"Yeah, we can do that. But be warned, if you keep spouting shit the way you have been just now, don't expect much sympathy from me." Chad's bluntness is both a blessing and a curse. Perhaps the fact that he's going to berate me is part of the draw to a night out with him. I barely recognize the man I'm becoming and I don't like it one bit.

"Wouldn't expect anything less," I quip. "I'll meet you at The Dane in about thirty minutes." We hang up and I glance over my shoulder before making a U-turn in the middle of the block.

Austin

Why don't you stay with Bree tonight? Something has come up and I don't know what time I will be done.

This time, I don't stop myself and my phone goes flying across the room. "Motherfucker!" I scream when I see my phone in three pieces in the corner.

"What's wrong?" Bree rushes out of the bathroom with one towel around her body and another wrapped in a turban on her head.

"David wants me to stay here tonight. I have no fucking clue what happened, but we were supposed to have plans today, and he hasn't talked to me since that bullshit earlier." I slump back on the sofa, scolding myself when I feel like crying again. I really thought I was doing the right thing, but as always, I should have done the opposite of what I wanted to do. "And whatever happened when he met with the department head, it was bad enough he can't even give me the courtesy of calling me to tell me to fuck off; he had to send a text message."

"Oh, honey," Bree purrs, sitting down next to me without bothering to get dressed. I suppose that's the benefit of being shoved in the 'gay best friend' box; she doesn't have to worry about covering up around me. "This clusterfuck has been stressful for both of you. I don't think he meant anything by it, and I think it'll do both of you some good to have a night apart. You've been hot and heavy since the word go, and that type of heat is hard to maintain. Let me get dressed and we'll run down for something to eat and gorge ourselves while watching cheesy chick flicks."

"You do realize that not every gay man loves that shit, right?" I ask, poking her in the side. I keep taunting her as she runs out of the room to put on clothes because it's better than throwing my arms around her and telling her how much her friendship means to me. I'm still not comfortable with that touchy-feely crap.

"Aww, come on! You're the only person I can rope into watching them. If you're nice, I'll even share my tissues. Trust me, it's what you're supposed to do when you're on the verge of or already dealing with a breakup."

I fall into the ratty chair that's behind me, thankful for its presence because otherwise I'd be on the floor. I'm not on the verge of a breakup, am I?

"You know what, Bree? I appreciate the offer, but I think I'm going to head home," I tell her, grabbing my bag from next to the door.

"Really?" she asks, the words muffled as she pulls a sweatshirt over her head.

"Yeah," I say firmly, portraying confidence I don't actually possess. "David gave me this long speech the other day about how we need to talk to one another. He was all sorts of pissed off that I didn't want to tell him what Rob said in class and the asshole actually made me believe that we could get through just about anything if we just talked to one another.

"Well, now he's going to get what he fucking wished for." I slide my feet into my shoes and dig through my pockets, hoping I have money on me for the bus. When I come up empty handed, Bree hands me two dollars without me having to ask. "If he's so pissed that he doesn't want to deal with me anymore, he's going to be man enough to tell me to my face. But you can be damn sure he's going to listen to me as well."

Bree kisses my cheek as she hugs me tightly. "I'm

so proud of you. I feel like your mama, puffing out my chest because you're finally growing up."

"Fuck off," I retort. "I grew up a while ago, just needed to get my head out of my ass. Don't drink a bottle of wine and pass out tonight because I might need to crash on your couch."

"I highly doubt it, but I promise I'll be here if you need me. Now, go before you chicken out." Bree laughs as she pushes me out the door. "And you'd better be here tomorrow either way to let me know how it goes!"

"Will do," I assure her, waving over my head as I walk out the door at the base of the stairs.

David

By ten o'clock, two facts are irrefutable: my car is going to have to stay here tonight and I am a moron when it comes to relationships. Chad wasn't lying when he said he wasn't going to go easy on me. Since the moment he sat down with the first pitcher of beer, he's been pointing out all the ways that I am book smart and life stupid.

"Face it, David, you've been walking around with blinders on ever since I met you," Chad slurs, sloshing beer on the table as he fills our glasses. We've had plenty to drink, but the alcohol seems to be hitting him much harder than it is me. I flag down our waitress to order some appetizers. "And all of a sudden, this cocky little shit waltzes into the room and you can't get out from under his spell."

I snort inelegantly, taking a long drink of my beer. "I can't disagree with you, but I don't think it's a matter of being under some sort of spell. I am still capable of freewill."

"Never said you weren't," Chad points out. "Doesn't change the fact that I'm not sure that kid could ever do anything to make you leave and that pisses you off because normally you'd kick someone to the curb for putting your job in jeopardy in any way."

He's right. My dedication to my career is at least a small part of why I have never pursued a serious relationship until now. Putting any part of my life in someone else's hands was more than I could allow. And I'm annoyed with myself because the first time I let my guard down, I went and fell in love with a man who brings more complications than anyone I have ever been involved with.

"So what do I do?" I ask pathetically.

Chad shrugs and leans back as the waitress fills our small table with plates of greasy food. He dives in, eating as if he's never seen food before. "I think it all comes down to answering one simple question," he mumbles around a mouth full of food.

"What's that?" I ask, staring at him as if he's my personal relationship mentor.

"Do you love him?" he asks, emphasizing every word.

Of course I love him. If I didn't, I would be better able to make a decision about that fate of our relationship. But we have reached an impasse and I'm unsure whether or not we'll get past it. "Yes," I respond, my voice steady because there's no question about how I feel.

"Then you need to learn to take the good with the bad," he advises me. "Do you think Becky and I get along all the time? I think she'd wonder what was wrong with me if I didn't piss her off at least twice a week. The thing is, we love each other enough that we don't let the problems drive a wedge between us."

"How did you decide that she's the one who was worth it?"

Chad gets a dopey look on his face and I can practically hear the gears grinding in his head. "Easy, she's the one person I couldn't imagine not seeing on a daily basis. When we were dating and she frustrated me, I would think about what my life would be like if she wasn't in it and I didn't like what I saw."

Although I don't have nearly the number of relationships behind me that he has, I completely understand what he's saying. All evening, I have been trying to convince myself that taking a break is the best solution to everything that has happened, but I can't fathom saying the words to Austin.

I toss a few bills on the table. "I hope you don't mind, but I think it's time for me to catch a cab and see if Austin will allow me to apologize."

"Attaboy," Chad says, slapping me on the back. "And if he won't listen tonight, try again tomorrow. Trust me, you're talking to someone who's made fucking up a part-time job. You have to realize it doesn't always work the first time you try to make amends."

"Thank you, Chad. Tell Becky I owe her dinner sometime soon." I rush outside, hoping it won't take too long to get downtown so I can take Austin home where he belongs.

I throw cash at the driver before the taxi even pulls to the curb and I'm weaving my way up the block as soon as he stops. Never before have I been this determined to do something for myself. Talking to Chad has made me realize that my life will be empty if I push Austin away.

My breathing is labored by the time I reach the top step and am standing at the door to Bree's apartment. The music inside is blaring, so I pound furiously on the door to be heard over the noise.

"Jesus, Austin! I told you--" The door swings open and Bree gapes at me, obviously expecting it to be person I'm here to see. "Oh, David. I wasn't expecting to see you tonight."

"That's understandable. I'm assuming Austin isn't here?" I ask, not failing to notice the way Bree is blocking my view of the interior of her apartment. She's making it abundantly clear that not only was she not expecting me, I'm not welcome in her home.

"No, he left a while ago." She offers no further information and I'm left staring at the door when she closes it in my face. I reach for my phone as I head outside, trying to figure out where he might have gone. When I dial Austin's number, it goes directly to voicemail. I plead with him to call me when he gets my message, but I doubt he will check it tonight. Rather than flag down the first taxi I see, I walk toward campus, hoping Austin is sitting in the park or down at the mall. It's a longshot, but he's been known to go to one of those two places when he wants to blend in with the crowd and forget about his problems for a while.

An hour later, I give up my hunt and slide into the back of a cab. Between the adrenaline, exercise and time, I wish I had my car because I'm completely sober at this point. I tell the driver to drop me off at The Dane so I don't have to deal with that in the morning. It also guarantees I won't be stranded if Austin decides to call me tonight and is willing to talk.

Chapter Twenty-One

Austin

The clock on the nightstand says it's almost one in the morning by the time I hear the front door close. I've spent the past few hours sorting through all of my belongings the way I wished I had at the end of last school year. I'm hoping there's no need for it, but if Bree was right and this is the end of David and me, I'm going to be better prepared this time. It's amazing how much crap I've accumulated that means nothing to me now.

"What's going on in here?" David asks when he walks into the room. I turn around and nearly crumble at the panicked look on his face. He rushes to close the distance, coming to an abrupt halt a few feet away from me. "Austin, we need to talk."

When used in that order, I'm pretty sure those are the four worst words in the English language. Hearing them from David, after the way he ignored me most of the day, reignites my anger.

"Oh, *now* you want to talk?" I sneer, squaring my shoulders as I cross my arms over my chest. "I fucking begged you to hear me out earlier today and you hung up on me. I can't even count the number of times I tried calling you, only to be ignored. You sure as shit talk a good game about the importance of communication, but from where I'm standing, it seems you only mean that when *you* want to talk."

"You're right," David says solemnly. "I don't blame you for being upset with me--"

"Do. Not. Patronize. Me." I practically spit out each word. My blood pressure spikes to the point I can hear it rushing through my head. "Plain and simple, David, this time you're the one who ran. You say how I don't trust you and I run from my problems, but that goes both ways. If you really trust me, if you actually love me, you can't run when I do stupid shit. I'm young. I'm inexperienced. I'm bound to fuck up. A lot. But you have to trust me that I would never go out of my way to do something that could harm you in any way."

David places his hands on my shoulders, backing me up until I'm sitting on the bed. He shoves a pile of my books to the floor so he can sit down beside me. My body is rigid, but I allow him to hold me as he speaks.

"Austin, you will never understand how sorry I am for how I behaved today. There's nothing I can say other than I'm sorry, and that doesn't seem like enough." I hate how easy it is for him to crack my resolve as he cards his fingers through my hair. After a quick kiss to my temple, he continues. "You may be young, but I guarantee that has no bearing on whether or not you are capable of being in a healthy relationship. I'm a thirty-six year old man who doesn't have much more experience than you do. And just like you, I'm going to misstep at times. But at the end of the day, the only thing that matters is if we are able to overcome our mistakes."

"I hear what you're saying, but I don't know if it's going to work that way," I admit. "What happens the next time something happens and one of us gets this upset? I honestly don't know if I can do this too many more times before I break. And as much as I love you, I've finally learned that I have to love myself even more."

Peace washes over me as I realize the truth of those words. It's because of David that I love myself for the first time in my life. My worth can no longer be determined by someone else's assessment of me. And I refuse to revert to the kid who would do just about anything to win the approval of others so I feel like I am a good person.

"I'm happy to hear you say that," David praises, burying his nose in the crook of my neck. "The thing is, when I think about my life without you in it, I realize that I don't ever want to know that ache again. I didn't know that I was incomplete before you, but I do now. That has nothing to do with my self-worth and everything to do with the fact that I'm a better man for having you by my side. If you can honestly tell me you don't feel the same way, I will have to accept that and let you go. But if you feel as I do, I believe we owe it to one another to promise that we'll never do this again."

I move so I'm sitting on David's lap with my arms around his waist. I untuck his button-down shirt and allow my fingers to work their way higher on his back. "David, I can't even tell you how much I love you. When I thought I might have cost you your job, or at the very least gotten you in trouble, I hated myself.

And that only got worse when you wouldn't talk to me. I feel like I had a glimpse of not having you in my life and it sucked big time. I'm willing to put in the effort if you are."

"You have no clue how happy that makes me." With his hands on my hips, David slides back on the bed and positions me so I'm straddling his lap. I grind against him, desperate to see what all the hype is about with make-up sex. "I can't say I will never mess up, but I can promise you I won't put you through what I did today ever again. If either of us feels like we aren't in a position to talk to the other, we need to have faith to be able to say that and know the other will give us space."

"I can deal with that," I tell him, leaning in to nip my way along his jaw up to his ear. "Can we kiss and make up now?"

David laughs and the amazing sound echoes off the walls. He falls back on the bed taking me with him. We strip one another with frantic need, biting and sucking any skin we can get our mouths on. And the entire time, we promise each other that this is only the beginning.

Epilogue

Austin

Four years later

Looking out over the first floor from the loft that will be my office, I can't believe today is actually here. Knowing that I'm going to be able to make a difference in one person's life is mind-blowing. And in a sick and twisted way, it's all because of my father. I'm sure he's rolling over in his grave right now, knowing that the trust fund he set up for me has been used to help homeless young adults get back on their feet.

"It looks amazing," David gushes as he steps up behind me. "I can't begin to tell you how proud I am of everything you've accomplished."

I turn to face my husband and I'm rendered speechless by the broad grin on his face. Some days, I thought I would drive him crazy with my obsession with the halfway house. As it is, he wound up calling Amanda and begged her to take over the wedding plans with Bree so I wasn't trying to take on too much at one time.

This may be my dream, but none of it would have been possible without my family, both by blood and by choice. Chad essentially donated the time and talent of his company to renovated an old Victorian home close enough to downtown that we'll be in a convenient location for those who need us most. Amanda and Tyler moved to Madison after she graduated from the University of Minnesota so she could run the business operations. Bree will be working with us as an art therapist as soon as she finishes school in May. And David, well it goes without saying that he's been vital to every aspect of this project.

"Thanks, babe. Now, I just hope people realize that we're here and it's okay to ask for someone to help them," I say, thinking about Casey for probably the millionth time since we closed on the house. I see him from time to time, still hanging out at the park, still struggling to get his feet under him. And still too fucking proud to realize that it's a sign of incredible strength to admit you can't do it on your own.

"We already have three guys moving in later today, so I don't think you have too much to worry about there," David reminds me. "And I truly believe you will find a way to reach out to those who need you and make them see that they aren't destined to a life of poverty because of their circumstances. That's what sets Jupiter House apart from every other shelter out there. You don't just want to help these men and women, you can relate to them."

I lay my head on David's chest, enjoying the last moments of peace we will have for the foreseeable future. Until we are able to hire more counselors, he and

I will be living in the loft most of the time and if the new residents are anything like I was at their age, it's bound to be a bumpy road.

David tilts my chin up and seals his lips over mine in a passionate kiss. I cup his ass, pulling him close enough to grind my thickening cock against his. This right here, this is what I've missed with as busy as we've both been. I miss the quiet time showing David with my body just how much I love him.

"God, would you two get a room?" Bree whines. It doesn't surprise me that I didn't hear her coming up the stairs, but it does say something about how distracted David was by what we were doing.

"In case you haven't noticed, you're in our room," David points out. "So if you don't want to see me sharing a moment with my husband, I suggest you turn your scrawny ass around and we'll see you downstairs."

"You know, I think I liked you better when you were all proper and shit," Bree responds. "Now, you're starting to remind me of Austin and that ain't right."

"Bree, was there something you needed?" I ask, wanting to deal with her and get her out of here so I can get back to molesting David.

"Yeah, I wanted to let you know that Oliver is waiting down in the intake office. Do you want me to show him to his room?" The selfish part of me wants to scream yes and shove her out of the room, but I can't do that. This is my place and I made a vow to be there for the residents. I groan, knowing there's only one right answer.

"No, I'll take care of him. You go down to the kitchen and ask the moms if everything is set for the reception after the ribbon cutting," I instruct her. I still think it's ridiculous to have all this pomp when the money could have been spent on shit that will directly benefit the house, but Amanda insisted. According to her, the media attention will help her secure donations from local companies, which is the ultimate goal, so we can keep the lights on indefinitely. Once we gave our moms permission to go nuts on a small reception for after the ceremony, they ran with it and I'm sure it'll be amazing.

"And you," I say, pointing at David. "We're not finished yet. I don't care how many times Chad asks, we are not going out with him tonight."

I straighten my shirt as I make my way through the great room, promising to catch up with everyone who is already gathering for the ceremony. But right now, there's a man who reminds me so much of myself it's scary sitting in the office waiting to be welcomed home.

"Oliver, it's great to see you again," I say as I sit in the chair next to him. I reach for a clipboard to start the last of the intake paperwork. David thought it would look more professional if I had a desk in here, but that's not what I'm going for. I want everything within these walls to feel approachable and welcoming because the people we're helping don't need more reminders of the gap between them and us. I don't want there to *be* a gap, although I know that's too much to ask for.

"We just have to get a bit more information and then I will show you to your room. I do have to remind you, life isn't going to be easy in here. There will be a schedule to adhere to and expectations to be met. Does that work for you?"

"Yes, sir. I don't want to be here any longer than I absolutely have to," he responds quickly, flinching when he realizes how that might sound. "Sorry, I just mean--"

"Oliver, I totally understand what you're saying. And please, call me Austin." We continue through to the end of the questionnaire and I set the paperwork aside. "Now, how about we get you settled? It's going to be crazy around here this afternoon, but everyone should be out by about six at the latest. Then, we'll have a low key night."

"Sounds good. I'm just happy to know where I'm going to sleep tonight." Oliver grabs his bag and follows me out of the office.

Oliver slams into my back when I stop short at the sight in front of me. Jordan, one of the other three men set to move in today is sitting in the hall waiting his turn. Next to him is the one man I never expected to see walk through the front door. "Casey, it's good to see you."

Standing this close, he looks tired and old beyond his years. "Hey, Austin. I...uh...I guess what I'm trying to say is..."

I save him from having to swallow the last remaining sliver of his pride. "Wait here with Jordan and we'll start the paperwork when I get back from showing Oliver to his room."

"Thanks, man. Whatever you need from me, I'm ready." Casey can't bring himself to make eye contact, but that's okay. Despite the fact that we've drifted over the years, there's no doubt that single sentence was harder for him to utter than anything else he's ever said.

"That's great." I hold Casey tight, silently promising to help him the same way he helped me years ago. I thought today couldn't get any better, but I was wrong.

Author's Note

Visit me at my website:
http://authorsloanj.com

If you enjoyed Teach Me, I would love it if you let your friends know so they can experience the relationship of Austin and David as well! As with all of my books, I have enabled lending on all platforms in which it is allowed to make it easy to share with a friend.

If you leave a review for Teach me on the site from which you purchased the book, Goodreads or your own blog, I would love to read it! Email me the link at authorsloanj@gmail.com and I will be sure to get in touch with you to thank you!

Other titles by Sloan Johnson:

Unexpected Angel
Unexpected Protector
Unexpected Consequences
Truth or Dare
Dare to Dream
Fragile Bonds

Make sure you never miss a new release or special offer announcement by signing up for Sloan's newsletter.

Godsend

An M/M Contemporary Romance
Coming Spring 2015

*A*nyone who claims death is easy has never died. For the past three-hundred sixty-three days, my mother has cried her way through her daily routine. She hasn't told my father, but the only time she eats anymore is when they're together. I've heard her screaming in the night, begging for God to take her now that her reason for living is gone. That saddens me because I always thought of my parents as the couple that all marriages should be modeled after, but that's no longer enough for her.

Daddy seems to know more than he's letting on, but like her, he's ignoring the pain. He'll spend part of every morning trying to talk to her, but winds up in his basement workshop before noon every day, only to be seen again at dinnertime.

True to his word, Daddy has been the rock of the family. He drove to our house on Christmas and forced Scott into his boots, saying he didn't care if my husband was wearing holey sweatpants and a stained shirt. Shelly would kick your ass if she knew that this is what you've become, *Daddy scolded him.*

Daddy's right. If I could do more than sit here and watch those I left behind fall apart, I'd do it. I'd like to say that day was a wake-up call for Scott, but I would be lying. Honestly, at that time, no one could blame him for turning into a hermit. He'd gone from having me there with him every day for over a decade to living on his own for the first time in his life. But now, it's gone on too long and I'm hoping Daddy remembers the promise he made me less than an hour before I died...

Scott

As I stack another box along the wall of the master bedroom, I stumble when I hear someone pounding on the front door. I regain my footing and go back to organizing, figuring if I'm quiet, whoever it is will go the fuck away. My Land Rover is hidden in the garage, so unless they go snooping, they'll have no way of knowing I'm inside.

The knocking stops and I breathe a sigh of relief. I know I'm being an asshole, but I can't bring myself to deal with any of the few people who would stop by unannounced. I've spent almost three months ignoring my father-in-law's phone calls, a fact which does make me feel more than a bit guilty, but I'm finally in the home stretch. One way or the other, I won't have to deal with all of this shit after tonight.

I stop what I'm doing and trudge down the stairs, carefully avoiding the mirror propped up against the wall in the downstairs hallway. I don't need to see my reflection to know that I look like shit. It's been at least four days since I shaved and I can't remember the last time I went for a haircut. It doesn't much matter since I rarely leave the house. If anything, it helps because no one dares to get too close when I look like a bum.

Reaching into the cupboard above the fridge, I realize there's a problem. There is only one bottle of tequila left, and it's the cheap shit. That wouldn't have happened when Shelly was alive; she would have made sure we had everything anyone could want to drink in the cabinet. She was the one who paid attention to things like being a good hostess. Then again, if I don't answer the door, he don't have to worry about entertaining, at which point it didn't much matter what I have on-hand.

I pour a healthy serving of the amber liquid into a rocks glass and tossed it back like a shot, slamming the glass on the counter for effect. I repeat the process two more times before getting pissed at myself for being so fucking weak. I hurl the glass across the room, feeling a strange satisfaction at the both the hole in the wall and the shards strewn across the granite floor. There will be time to regret my outburst in the morning, but for now, there is tequila to drink. I lift the bottle to my mouth and chug.

The alcohol loses its flavor as a good drunk sets in just about the same time the pounding on the door resumes. I stand in the middle of the kitchen, not daring to move an inch in case whoever it is tries peering in the window beside the door. "Scott Andrew Murphy, I know you're in there! You've hidden away long enough, it's time to be the man she believed you to be," Jim Pryce shouts from the other side of the door.

I clench my fists, gearing up for a good fight with the man who once called me his son. I storm to the front door, throwing it open with such force that it bounces off the wall, taking down a coat rack in the process. "When you've been through what I have this past year, then you can insult me. Until then, you have no fucking right to come to my house and lecture me."

I'm not a small man by any stretch of the imagination, but Jim has at least three inches on my six foot frame. "You little shit! I know you're hurting, but have you turned so far into yourself that you don't realize how hard Shelly's death has been on all of us? No, my wife didn't die, but Shelly was my child. My only child. Do you know what it's like to wake up every morning knowing that the little girl I raised is never coming back?

"I made her a promise the day she died, and I've felt guilty every single day I let you ignore my calls because I wasn't doing what she asked of me." Jim digs his hands into my shoulders and proceeds to push me into the living room. The older man growls when he lays eyes on the piles of unopened mail, take-out containers and other garbage strewn around the room. After shoving me down onto the couch, Jim disappears into the kitchen, returning with a large black garbage bag.

"I've tried to give you some space because I wasn't about to tell you how to grieve, but dammit, Scott, it's time for this shit to end," he scolds as he scoops the obvious garbage into the bag. "You'll probably always miss her, but what would she say if she saw you looking like you do? Or if she could walk in that door and see her house looking like the city dump? She'd hate what you've done to yourself since she left."

The truth of those words hits me right in the gut. Another round of tears boils to the surface, rendering me incapable of doing anything other than doubling over to cry. "I just...I feel like I'm lost now that she's gone," I sob. "I'd give anything to have another day, another chance to tell her how much I love her. She was my entire life for eleven years and my best friend even longer."

Jim pulls me into his side, holding me while I fall apart completely. This complete breakdown is one that's been a year coming and I don't even feel bad about showing my weakness in front of my father-in-law. He's a better man than I deserve, letting me scream at him and accuse him of not understanding what I'm going through. Truthfully, I feel as though I've failed him in some way by not being there to help Shelly's parents through their grief.

Once my body stops convulsing with the power of my tears, Jim releases me and begins cleaning the living room while I sit on the couch, dazed and barely seeing anything.

"Scott, I know how much Shelly meant to you, but what do you think she would say if she saw how you're letting yourself go now that she's gone?" Jim asks as he sorts through my mail. "She and I talked a lot in the months leading up to... well, in those last few months. And her biggest fear was that you would do exactly what you are now. I know it hurts, but you have to live. If nothing else, live for her. She may be gone, but now it's up to you to live the life she wanted and can never have."

His words twist the knife in my heart, mostly because he's right. Shelly always wanted the best for everyone. The biggest kick in the balls with all of this is the fact that she's the one I turned to for nearly twenty years when I was upset because she had this way of making it impossible to be in a bad mood around her. Now, I have to figure out how to cope without her by my side.

"I guess you're right," I concede, scrubbing my overgrown stubble. Another hundred pounds of guilt lands on my heart when I think about what I had considered a viable option for processing my guilt up until about ten minutes ago.

I'm not sure I will ever have the balls to admit it to Jim or anyone else, but had he not shown up when he did, I knew with unwavering certainty that I was either going to run away and never look back or end my own life so I could be with Shelly again. And the fucked up part is I tried to justify the latter by telling myself it would be no worse than what she did. But it is, because physically I am a strong, healthy man, it's only my emotional state that is weak and ailing.

"Of course I'm right," Jim chuckles, the sound so out of sync with the sadness behind his eyes it startles me. At least he can bring himself to pretend that he's okay. "After all, a lot of what I've said comes straight from what Shelly told me to tell you, and we both know she was the smart one in the family. Now, why don't you go up and take a shower while I clean up down here. There's somewhere I think you need to be."

I consider protesting, but I owe this to Shelly and her parents. Someday, I will thank Jim for both giving me time to grieve and for being so adamant about figuring out how to live again.

Sitting in the cold, stark commons room in the basement of city hall, I'm beginning to question Jim's insistence on attending a group grief counseling session. The way everyone greeted him when we walked in, it was apparent that he's a frequent visitor here. I wonder if he's said anything about me to the members of the group with the way no one holds eye contact with me when I catch them looking my way.

"I'd like to thank everyone for coming tonight," the leader says as she weaves through the small groups gathered around the room. All conversation ceases as everyone quickly finds a seat. "It's great to see so many of you were able to join us tonight, and it's always wonderful to see a few new faces."

She nods my direction and offers me a friendly smile. I nod slightly, hoping she's not about to force me to stand and tell everyone about myself and why I'm here. I don't want to talk about Shelly or the fact that she's gone; every detail about our love and loss is seared into my heart and mind. Talking to Jim and talking to complete strangers are two totally different things. As though he knew I was thinking about him, Jim clamps his hand on my shoulder, giving it a reassuring squeeze.

"For those who haven't been here before, please know that we understand how hard it is to walk through the doors the first time," she continues. "Everyone in this room has been through a loss, but every situation is completely unique. You will never hear anyone in this group tell you they know how you feel, nor will we expect you to grieve in a certain way.

"We don't believe in forcing anyone to share information they aren't ready to, but please be aware that you will get the best results out of your time here if you do eventually open up. After all, the first step to letting go of the pain is addressing the pain." I roll my eyes, already sick of the sunshine and rainbows flying around the room.

Jim nudges me when I start to zone out while the leader discusses ways to reinvest in life after the loss of a loved one. I blink hard a few times to try to focus on what she's trying to say, but my mind keeps wandering to those last days with Shelly when she pleaded with me to go on with my life after she was gone.

"Does anyone have anything they'd like to add?" the leader prods when she's finished with her prepared topic. A few people raise their hands, including the man siting directly to my left. Suddenly, I'd love nothing more than to hear what everyone else in the room has to say, just so there won't be time for Jim to share his feelings.

The next twenty minutes are spent listening to those who are further on their 'path to recovery' (who coined that ridiculous term?) tell those of us who are just starting to live again all about how life will eventually get better. Some of the suggestions are beyond ridiculous, but I sit a bit straighter and pay attention when one guy chimes in and says that sitting in group isn't always the answer.

"What makes you say that, Chris?" she asks defensively. Honestly, I'm shocked she didn't shoot him down since this guy basically told her that it's pointless for any of us to be here.

The guy, Chris, leans forward in his seat, resting his elbows on his knees. I'm transfixed as I watch him tuck a stray lock of blond hair behind his ear. I've never been attracted to guys with long hair, but there's something about the way his waves fall right to the edge of his square jawline that make me want to be the one running my fingers through his hair to see if it's as soft as it looks.

As I wait for him to answer the question, I take mental note of every inch of him, from his worn cowboy boots, to the way his jean hug his thighs. His black t-shirt and blazer almost seem out of place with the casual look on the lower half of his body, but somehow, he manages to pull it off.

"Well, I mean, it's not all bad, but let's think about this logically for a moment," he counters, a slight smirk showing at the corner of his mouth. "You just spent the first thirty minutes telling us how important it is that we move on, that we 'invest' in our own lives instead of dying along with our loved ones." I hide my snort of laughter behind a cough when he makes air quotes as he talks, essentially mocking her topic for the evening.

"And yeah, right now we're talking about how we can or can't relate to what you said, but next, you're going to ask us all how we're feeling this week." Chris grows more animated as he speaks and everyone gives him their undivided attention. A few seem appalled by his audacity, but others gently nod their heads in agreement. "I can tell you, most people in this room are feeling pretty shitty. We're lonely and sad and life sucks a lot of the time. Sitting here singing kumbaya and holding hands week after week, month after month, isn't going to change the fact that some days it's almost too much work to get out of bed."

Finally, a voice of reason, all wrapped up in one hell of an attractive package. It's the first time since Shelly that I've dared admire someone's looks and the guilt I feel is for not feeling worse than I do. Perhaps that's because it wasn't something that was off-limits, even before Shelly got sick the last time. She knew who I was when we met and I never hid those feelings from her, so it doesn't feel like a betrayal now, which causes me to question how I could think about someone while I'm sitting next to the father of the woman I pledged my life to.

"I suppose that's an interesting perspective, Chris," the leader concedes. "And yet, you've been here every week for the past four months. Why do you suppose that is?"

"Be damned if I know," Chris huffs, slouching a bit in his seat. "Maybe because sometimes it's nice to know I'm not alone."

Acknowledgements

And now, for the hardest pages of the book. I know I say it every time I finish a project, but there are so many people who help me on the path from a rough idea to a completed book that I know I will never remember every single person. If you're not on here and know that you've helped me in some way, please accept my apologies and tell me to buy you a drink when I see you!

First and foremost, a huge thank you goes out to Kristen and Nikki. Somehow, I have been blessed with two of the best friends a girl could ever ask for. You keep me sane when I want to scream or cry, you tell me to shut up when I doubt myself, and you tell me to fix it when I suck. I'm not sure I will ever be able to wrap my head around the fact that you ladies are in my life. I can't wait until the next time we can all hole up in a hotel room and laugh until we cry (among other things...).

Jackie, you put up with so much from me as I wrote this book. You were my safety net and my cheerleader. Every person who touches this book should thank you because you wouldn't let good enough be good enough on any page.

Ena and Jennifer, what you ladies do to help me promote is a true blessing. Thank you for being there when I need you!

Anna, thank you for being there to answer random questions and for not punching me when I change my mind on when I need to send files to you and get them back!

There are so many bloggers I need to thank for supporting me that I won't even begin to list them because I *will* forget someone important. What you ladies (and a few gents) do for myself and all authors is truly astounding. You don't get paid to promote our work, there's nothing for you to gain, and yet you take time away from your "real lives" to help us succeed. You're our cheerleaders when we're down and our sounding boards when you're upset. I think just about every author out there would agree that without you, there's no way any of us would be where we are.

And last, but most definitely not least... thank you to my amazing family. Rick, you've been on this roller coaster with me for over two years now and I really do need to thank you for doubting me early on. You upset me enough that it pushed me to get through my first book, then the next and then the one after that. It wasn't easy in the beginning, but now, you are my everything when it comes to my career just as much as you are in the rest of my life.

Bubba and Mack, you are, without question, the two most amazing kids a mother could ask for. How I got so lucky to have you as mine, I will never know. Mommy loves you both very much!

Made in the USA
Middletown, DE
17 March 2015